I Promise To …

Zoe Burton

I Promise To...

Zoe Burton

Published by Zoe Burton

© 2014 Zoe Burton/Sweet Escapes Press

Early drafts were written and posted serially in June 2014.

ISBN: 978-1-953138-21-7

Acknowledgements

First, I thank Jesus Christ, my Savior and Guide, without whom this story would not have been told. I love you!

Additional thanks go to my betas and cold readers: Rose, Aino, and Sarah, and to my proofreader: Eileen. You ladies rock!

Chapter 1

Elizabeth Bennet Darcy, age seven and ten and held securely in her husband's arms, lay dreaming on the eve of her first wedding anniversary. Like all dreams, this one jumped around from event to event. Unlike other dreams, this one featured her husband and herself at various times in their lives. It was as if her life had been made into a drama on the stage at a Covent Garden theater, complete with narrator …

~~~***~~~

George Darcy and Edward Gardiner sat in Mr. Gardiner's office in his warehouse in Cheapside, discussing their latest business venture. Mr. Darcy had met and become an investor in Mr. Gardiner's import/export business three years ago, following the death of his wife. The venture had greatly prof-
~~~

ited both men. From that beginning, a friendship developed. Mr. Darcy respected Mr. Gardiner's incredible business acumen, and Mr. Gardiner respected his largest investor's ability to overlook social norms and befriend a mere tradesman.

Unlike some other members of the landed gentry, Mr. Darcy knew in his heart that their way of life would one day change. New inventions were beginning to be developed which would likely someday completely alter it. Land ownership was still vitally important, but a prudent gentleman did not put his eggs all in one basket. These new inventions had already drawn some of his tenants away from the estate. He knew that he – or his son, should he himself pass before it happened – could potentially wake one morning to find he had no tenant farmers left at all. Even barring that event, the land was dependent on the weather. A too-dry or too-wet year could devastate profits, and while Darcy had an impressive fortune, that money would not last forever. A wise man knew to earn his income from more than one place; investment into the future was the way to go.

As the two gentlemen carried on their discussion, the office door was suddenly flung open and in rushed a petite little ten-year-old girl with long brown curls. "Uncle, Uncle!" cried the young lady. "Fitzwilliam called me a hoyden! What is a hoyden, Uncle?"

The question was still being asked as a lanky young gentleman a mere five years older than the girl rushed into the room and came to a quick standstill. He had hoped to catch her before she got to her uncle, as he knew the gentlemen were still meeting. His heart sank as he realized she had beaten him. He should have reacted faster.

"Fitzwilliam! We do not call names, son. I am disappointed; you know better." George Darcy's reprimand was a hard blow to his son. The respect of his father was something he always craved. That did not stop him from trying to defend himself, though.

"But Father, she was climbing into the crates of goods!" The young man's hand waved in the direction of the warehouse floor.

"It does not matter what Miss Elizabeth did or did not do. She is a lady, regardless of her actions today. She is young, and at times, young people do things they ought not. That does not make her a hoyden." Darcy was severe with his son in this instance. Fitzwilliam needed to learn that making sport of someone was not acceptable behavior for a Darcy.

"Yes, Father. I understand. I will not repeat my mistake."

"You will apologize to Miss Elizabeth," replied his father, nodding his approval.

Fitzwilliam did not wish to apologize to the hoy- … girl, but to please his father he would, and he would mean it. Nor did he desire a more severe punishment, as George Darcy was known for suspending his riding privileges for grievous offenses, and young Fitzwilliam was ready to do what was necessary to prevent any interruption of his favored activity.

He turned to young Elizabeth. "I am sorry for calling you names, Miss Elizabeth."

Little Lizzy threw him a triumphant grin. "I accept your apology, Master Fitzwilliam."

Mr. Gardiner caught her look. "Do not think you are coming away from this without consequence, Miss Lizzy," he said.

Elizabeth's head spun towards her uncle, mouth hanging open.

"What have I told you about climbing into those crates?"

Fitzwilliam struggled to keep hidden the smirk that was threatening to spread over his lips. It looked like he was not the only one in trouble today.

Three years later

Gardiner's friendship with Darcy had grown right along with their business partnership. The gentlemen and their families were frequently together; dinner at one or the other's home, nights at the theatre, or even visits to the races at Epsom were common. Frequently in company with the group were the Gardiners' two eldest nieces, Elizabeth and Jane.

Jane was already quite the beauty. Blonde, graceful, and serene, at five and ten she drew the eyes of men. In her hometown of Meryton, her mother had put her "out" in society. Mrs. Bennet was highly concerned about what would happen to her five daughters should Mr. Bennet up and die one day. Since her eldest was the most beautiful of the lot, she was sure it would not take long for a rich man to snap her up. There were few of them in Meryton, especially unmarried gentlemen, so she shipped Jane off to London to spend the season with the Gardiners. Given her brother's friendship with the rich Mr. Darcy, Mrs. Bennet knew Jane would be exposed to many wealthy young men.

Elizabeth was another matter entirely. While not quite the wild child she was at ten, at three and ten Lizzy was rather awkward. She had grown a little taller, and overall she did not seem to quite fit together. She was now entirely too old for playing with the boys. However much she disliked it, Elizabeth must learn to master the accomplishments expected of the daughter of a gentleman. As a result, she was learning to embroider and sew and to play the pianoforte and sing.

Her father allowed her free rein in his library, and discussed with her the books she had read. As Elizabeth was a voracious reader and not shy about stating and defending her position on matters, the two had whiled away many an afternoon or evening in this manner.

Mrs. Bennet frequently fussed at both her second daughter and her husband. It simply would not do for Lizzy to be too educated. No gentleman wanted a wife who read too much. The occasional novel was acceptable; tomes on farm management and philosophy were not. Despite her repeated protests that with Elizabeth's unfortunate looks she would have a difficult enough time finding a husband without adding the unattractiveness of being too smart, Mr. Bennet continued to allow his daughter to read to her heart's content.

Lizzy's usual response to her mother's words was to discreetly roll her eyes and respond with a witty statement of some sort or other. However, the words did hurt. She knew she was not as beautiful as Jane and never would be, but her mama really did not need to continue to repeat it.

The Gardiners knew, of course, of Mrs. Bennet's opinion of her second daughter. They wholeheartedly disagreed with it, and often wondered how a mother could look at such a beautiful young lady and not see that beauty. For this reason, when Jane was sent to London for the season, Elizabeth was asked to come, too. Over the years, the couple had hosted both girls numerous times, most especially during Mrs. Bennet's confinements with her youngest daughters.

The Darcys' opinions on the Bennet girls matched the Gardiners'. While Jane was undoubtedly beautiful, the same could also be said of Elizabeth. The girl was still growing into her looks, of course, but she showed the promise of extreme external beauty to match the already sterling beauty inside.

Though younger than the sisters by a few years, Mr. Darcy's daughter, Georgiana, loved them like they were her sisters. The three were frequently found together playing with dolls, practicing the pianoforte, or studying Georgiana's lessons. Oftentimes, if the Gardiners were accompanying Jane to a ball or other function, Lizzy spent the night with Georgiana. The two girls looked forward to these times, Georgiana because she usually had no one to play with and talk to, and Elizabeth because Georgiana was such a wonderful person with whom to spend time.

In addition, the Gardiners spent a month each summer at Pemberley. They now had a standing invitation to visit whenever they were in Derbyshire. When at the estate, the girls' activities included many outdoor entertainments. They admitted Fitzwilliam to their group whenever he was of a mind to participate, which was usually when the activity involved the horses. It was he who taught Elizabeth to ride, a sometimes arduous process due to the fact that Lizzy did not appreciate being told what to do, and Fitzwilliam was just arrogant enough, at least in her mind, to expect her to do it.

During one of her visits, Elizabeth was injured in a minor accident. She was an excellent tree climber, much to her mother's dismay, and she had convinced Georgiana to scale a tree in the garden. The two were sitting on the lowest branch, in deference to Georgiana's lack of skill in the art, chatting about lessons and friends and all the things girls like to discuss. They became engrossed in conversation to the point that they did not see Fitzwilliam approach. The young gentleman thought it would be funny to climb up the other side of the tree and try to frighten the girls. Georgiana saw him out of the corner of her eye, and assumed Lizzy did, as well. However, when Fitzwilliam tapped them both on the shoulder and spoke, Elizabeth startled so badly that she lost her seat, falling off the limb and landing on her back. Immediately, Fitzwilliam scrambled down and raced to Elizabeth's side. She was so still that at first he thought she was dead, until suddenly her eyes opened and she gasped for breath.

Once he had ascertained that she was alive and relatively uninjured, he went back to help his sister down, before returning to Elizabeth's side. Georgiana ran to the house for her father; Fitzwilliam knelt beside Lizzy, holding her hand and talking to her. When she tried to sit up, he put his arm around her shoulder; and when she began to cry at the pain in her posterior, he held her close to his side, her hand in his, and crooned words of comfort to her. Elizabeth spent the rest of that summer's visit laying on her stomach in her room with only Georgiana, Mrs. Gardiner, and the maids for company.

The relationship between Fitzwilliam and Elizabeth was the one to catch the attention of both families. Both were great readers, and given Lizzy's willingness and ability to debate, they spent many hours challenging each other. At times, their rebuttals degenerated into arguments, and intervention by adults was sometimes required. Both were of a fiery disposition. But they were never able to stay angry with each other for long. Generally, by the end of the Gardiners' and Bennets' visit, the two were at least speaking to each other again.

Master Fitzwilliam's father and Miss Elizabeth's uncle and aunt were quite aware of the sparks that flew between their son and niece. The Gardiners vowed to keep a close watch on the situation, as it would not do for Lizzy to become attached to a young gentleman who could not or would not offer for her. Nor would it do for her mother to hear of it. The Gardiners shuddered to think of the scene that would arise in that case. Mr. Darcy, on the other hand, hoped, in the back of his mind, that he might one day see his son offer for such a fine young lady.

~~~***~~~

Elizabeth smiled in her sleep at such pleasant dreams and burrowed deeper into her husband's arms.
~~~

Chapter 2

Darcy House, London

Edward Gardiner stared at the front of George Darcy's desk while the gentleman perused the document describing the venture they were discussing. He could hear Mr. Darcy commenting on what he was reading, but Gardiner's mind was not in the room … it was on a problem at home.

"Gardiner, are you well? Gardiner? Gardiner!" Mr. Darcy's voice rose at the last, snapping the man's attention back to himself. "What is wrong? I have tried to gain your attention these ten minutes, at least."

Mr. Gardiner sighed. "I apologize. My mind was miles away."

"Is there anything I can do?" Darcy inquired.

Gardiner considered for a few minutes. Perhaps by sharing his trouble with his friend, a solution, even a temporary one, might be found. Certainly, Darcy had better contacts than he himself did. They had known each other for many years, having met during a business meeting. In light of their long friendship, his decision was made.

"I do have a problem. It involves my niece, Elizabeth. Her father has sent her to stay with us, for her own safety. It appears that her mother is pushing Lizzy into a courtship with a man. Lizzy does not want him, and according to my brother, the gentleman has been abusive to her.

"Bennet wrote that she left the house one afternoon to walk in the garden in an attempt to avoid this man. My brother noticed the gentleman follow her out and was uncomfortable with it. He was aware of the low regard Elizabeth holds for the man. When he reached the area where the couple was standing, he heard the gentleman ask for her hand and Lizzy refuse him. Bennet then heard her cry out, and rushed closer. This gentleman was gripping my niece's arm, and before Bennet could reach him, he had struck her several times with his closed fist. Bennet kicked the gentleman off his property and took Elizabeth into the house.

"Her mother is in an uproar, because Elizabeth refused the man. She is concerned about losing her home upon her husband's death, as the estate is entailed upon heirs male. Based on some of the things my sister has said when she did not know Bennet could hear, she will do anything, including setting up a compromise, for Elizabeth to marry this man. Bennet supports his daughter's decision not to wed the bounder. Elizabeth was rather severely injured in the attack, sustaining a broken cheekbone to go along with the bruising and swelling. She was bedridden for two weeks, during which time her mother repeatedly entered her room to berate and threaten her. Bennet finally made the decision to send her to me.

"My wife and I have enjoyed having Elizabeth with us this last month. Physically, she is much improved. The swelling in her face is gone, and the bruises are faded almost completely. Emotionally, she is wary of people, particularly men, but mostly those with whom she is not well acquainted. However, that is not our main concern. Her rejected suitor showed up on our doorstep last evening, demanding to see her. We refused him entrance, of course, which resulted in him becoming very angry and making threats. We are worried that we may not be able to keep her safe."

Mr. Darcy listened to the story in silence. When it appeared that Gardiner had run out of words, he began asking questions. "Did your brother Bennet call the magistrate and have this blackguard arrested?" Darcy could not imagine allowing someone to get away with committing a similar act against his daughter, Georgiana.

Mr. Gardiner responded, "He is afraid that such action will cause more problems. The gentleman involved is a peer."

"A peer? What is his name?

"Lord Regis."

"Oh, Gardiner … the gentleman has quite the reputation. I cannot imagine allowing him near my Georgiana. How can I help you in this? Because I do intend to help you. You know that I value Miss Elizabeth very highly."

George Darcy and his children had spent many enjoyable hours in Elizabeth Bennet's presence as she was growing up. He enjoyed her wit and her lively spirit. He was saddened to hear of her timidity now, as her strength and courage had always been one of the qualities he most enjoyed about her.

Mr. Gardiner's reply was sure and certain, "If you could help me figure out a way to keep her safe, I would be most grateful. The thought of Lizzy coming to any harm tears me up inside. I have sent one of the strong men from the warehouse to guard her when I am not there, but short of putting bars on the windows, I have no idea what else I can do. Thankfully, this episode has caused her to rethink the idea of walking out, so I have not had that worry. She stays indoors constantly unless she goes shopping with her aunt or on an outing with the family. What else can we do?"

It was Mr. Darcy's turn to ponder for a moment. "If you will allow me, I will hire men to guard the outside of your house. That will improve the situation greatly." Here he paused, gazing out the window and mentally reviewing options, as an idea formed in his mind. "I think the best solution is this: let us betroth Elizabeth and Fitzwilliam."

Mr. Gardiner's eyebrows shot up to his hairline.

"I know it is perhaps an unconventional way to protect her, but I have long believed that they are made for each other. Think of all the debates they have had and how much they have in common. His face lights up when he hears her name, and hers does the same when he walks into the room. I am not saying that they are in love. In fact, I am sure that if we were to ask each of them, they would deny it. However, my observations tell me differently, and were I to be wrong, I am certain that in time, they would fall in love.

"Too, by letting it be known that she is spoken for, we may be able to dissuade Lord Regis from his pursuit. In addition, Miss Elizabeth will be, for all intents and purposes, part of my family. It will be easier to protect her as such. What do you say?"

Gardiner was speechless. "Are you quite sure? I agree that Fitzwilliam and Elizabeth seem well-matched to each other, but she has little in the way of a dowry; just one thousand pounds on her mother's death. And while I know that we are friends, that is not the same as family. What will yours think of the connection to me? And what of Fitzwilliam? How will he react to this? And your sister-in-law, Lady Catherine … does she not want Fitzwilliam to marry her daughter?"

"Yes, I am quite sure about it. I understand your concerns, but I do not share them. My family is well-aware of our friendship and gave up squawking about it years ago. They will not even whimper about the marriage. To be honest, they all should have expected something like this, including my sister. To this point, I have not supported her desire, nor have I indicated to Fitzwilliam that he should or should not marry his cousin. To be frank, it is doubtful Anne would be able to bear him an heir, even if she had any accomplishments that might attract him.

"As for the dowry, the Darcys have more than enough money to go around. My investments with you have grown our income immensely. No, Gardiner, I have no reservations. My marriage was a love match, and was quite rare. They are still rare today. However, that is what I desire for my children.

"Miss Elizabeth and Fitzwilliam were formed for each other. One only has to observe them together to see it. It will do my heart good to know that they are together and thriving and that she is safe. One never knows what may happen in the future, and I would rather see my son in a happy marriage to someone who will love him than to leave it all to chance. Come; let us draw up the settlement. I will take it to my solicitor this afternoon, and write to my son.

"I know that he enjoys spending time with Elizabeth, and he will do his duty by me and obey me. His tour is wrapping up and he will return soon. At least with this blasted war, he is not far from home. When I went on my tour, I travelled all over the continent. His latest letter indicated he was enjoying the sport in the area of Dumfries and that he would be heading south by the time I received the missive."

"Indeed, Darcy; you have convinced me. Thankfully, when Bennet sent Lizzy to us, he gave me authority to act in his stead. We will not have to be concerned about getting his signature. He trusts me to do right by his favorite daughter. And yes, I will take a glass of that fine port you are waving around; I know you are about to ask." Gardiner and his friend shared a laugh before getting down to business.

The two gentlemen spent the next hour setting out the terms of Elizabeth's settlement. Gardiner was rather surprised at the generous terms Darcy was describing in the document. When questioned, however, George Darcy was adamant. His new daughter-in-law would be well-provided for and protected. Her beginnings may have been humble, but Darcy knew her true worth. Fitzwilliam would never be happy with a simpering lady from the *ton*, whose only concerns were for herself and her next shopping trip. Miss Elizabeth, he knew, cared little for material things. She valued his son as an intelligent young man, but she would keep him in check. He needed that, as he tended to be rather arrogant with those he considered socially inferior. That trait came from his mother's family; Fitzwilliam's maternal relations were insufferably so. The more Darcy thought about it, the more convinced he became that this was the right thing to do, for Fitzwilliam as well as Miss Elizabeth.

Chapter 3

Upon arriving home from his visit with Mr. Darcy, Gardiner took a deep breath before stepping into the parlor. He was not entirely sure how his niece would react to his news.

"Edward, you are home," exclaimed his wife, Maddie. "How was your meeting with Mr. Darcy?"

"Very productive, my dear. May I inquire about your day? And that of my lovely niece?"

"We had a wonderful time shopping today. We bought fabric and ordered gowns for our trip to the theatre." Here Mrs. Gardiner glanced anxiously at her niece. She was not sure how much Elizabeth had heard yesterday when their "visitor" made his claims. She was not even sure they were still going to the theater, but not wanting to alarm the girl unnecessarily, she kept the appointment with the modiste. Lizzy made no mention of the events and did not seem to be concerned about the upcoming theater visit.

Gardiner asked his wife for a private conference. "I have something on which I would like your opinion. Do you have a moment to come to my study?" The look he gave his wife let her know that whatever it was, it was important.

"Certainly, my dear. I will come with you now. Lizzy, will you be well here alone for a bit?"

"Yes," Elizabeth replied with a timid smile. "I will be here when you are finished." That said, she picked up the handkerchief she had been embroidering and set to work.

Maddie and Edward retreated to the study, where Gardiner quickly filled her in on his conversation and activities with George Darcy. Maddie was just as shocked by the news as her husband had been when it was first proposed to him earlier in the afternoon.

"What I really need to determine is how to tell Lizzy," Mr. Gardiner said. "You know how independent she can be, and I am not altogether certain of her feelings towards Fitzwilliam. I know she likes him well enough, but will she fight this marriage?"

"I do not know. Perhaps once we explain Lord Regis' presence here yesterday and our fears for her safety, she will agree. The degree of her happiness with the prospect I cannot predict," Maddie replied.

"Well, why do we not just get it done, then. Let us go talk to her now. We will have time during our meal to discuss her concerns."

Upon re-entering the parlor, Maddie went to sit beside Elizabeth while Mr. Gardiner claimed a chair on her other side. A look from her husband told Maddie that he wished her to begin. "Elizabeth, we have something we need to discuss with you."

Elizabeth immediately paled. "What is wrong?"

Maddie reached for her hand, then took a deep breath. "Lord Regis came here last night. Did you hear what he said?"

Elizabeth looked perplexed and wary. "I could not make out his words, but I could hear his voice. I was in the nursery with the children. They were very frightened. What did he say?"

"He threatened you, Lizzy. Not just you, but all of us. Your uncle and I spent much of last night discussing our options for keeping you safe. There is more," she said when it appeared that her niece was going to interrupt. "Your uncle visited Mr. Darcy today, on a matter of business. During the meeting, this subject came up between them, and Mr. Darcy presented a solution. Your uncle and I agree that this is the best path for us to take. We want you to know that we would not have agreed to this if your safety and happiness was not of paramount importance to us."

Elizabeth appeared to be contemplating all that she had heard, and indeed she was. Her aunt and uncle had brought up some valid points in their presentation. Among the most important to her was their safety, for it was true that they and her cousins were in just as much danger as she was. Did she truly desire to be the cause of injury to any of them? Most assuredly not!

"What was Mr. Darcy's solution, Uncle?"

Gardiner responded. "Firstly, he has hired men to guard the house from the outside, and plans to send over some of his burliest footmen to guard it from the inside. One will stay with you at all times, and one will stay by the door and only admit those we specify. The third will remain on duty upstairs. Their sole assignment is to keep you from harm, and by extension the rest of the family."

He took a deep breath. So far, Elizabeth had taken his news rather calmly, a clear statement of her unease. Now, however, he had come to the hard part. "The other solution Mr. Darcy presented was for you and his son to enter into an engagement and marriage. This will allow him to better aid us in keeping you safe."

Here he paused, looking carefully at Lizzy. He was not surprised when confusion, then shock, then anger chased across her features.

"You arranged a marriage for me? I have sworn my whole life to marry only for the deepest love, and you expect me to wed a man I have not seen in months? What are you thinking? Surely there must be another way! I could go away somewhere, to a place Lord Regis would never think to look. You must have connections enough to find me a place? ”

Almost as soon as she said those words, she knew in her heart that it was impossible, and her uncle and Mr. Darcy were right, but it grated that her choice was taken away. Marriage was probably the best solution. Still, to go into such an alliance without love! She sighed to herself.

“Lizzy,” her uncle began, with an urgency in his voice that made her take notice, “I beg of you, do not dismiss the notion out of hand. The Darcys' resources are far greater than ours, and with your marriage to Fitzwilliam they would be able to protect you. Even before the marriage, as his betrothed, he can acceptably provide a level of protection for you that I simply cannot manage. If I had not so recently expanded my warehouses, it may have been possible, but at this point, I do not have the extra funds. And you know you think well of him. The two of you share many of the same tastes, in books, the theater …"

Here Gardiner paused, then continued softly. "It is done already, my dear, and cannot be undone without great scandal and likely a vast amount of money. Mr. Darcy has already taken the settlement papers to his solicitor; the news is out. Your father entrusted me with your life and safety, and I will do whatever it takes to keep you safe, happy, and healthy."

Mrs. Gardiner had remained quiet to this point, but now felt compelled to add her own thoughts to the discussion. "Lizzy, you know your uncle is correct. You and Fitzwilliam are a good match. Please, dear niece, do not fight us on this. Look inside your heart; see the truth."

Elizabeth sighed. She knew they were correct, from a practical point of view. She did get along well with Fitzwilliam, and they did enjoy many of the same activities. She admired him a great deal. She was uncertain she loved him, and it was the throwing over of her desire to marry for love that gave her unease. What would happen to her if their regard for each other grew cold? She did not want a marriage like her parents had—cold and mocking. She wanted hers to be like the Gardiners'—loving and warm. At her aunt's urging, she shared her thoughts with them.

"What if we never grow to love one another, or if one of us grows to loathe the other? I would be miserable in a marriage like the one I see before me daily at Longbourn."

"Oh, my dear niece," her aunt responded. "I know you would, and there is no guarantee that it will not. But it might very well turn out to be exceedingly happy. Your uncle has already reminded you of the similarities between you and Fitzwilliam. Do you really think you could be so miserable with a man with whom you have so much in common? A gentleman whom you regard well? Your parents did not have such a foundation for their marriage. Your father, as I understand it, was so impressed with your mother's looks and vivacity that he never looked beneath the surface to see if there was any substance. You and Fitzwilliam already know you are compatible.

"As much as it pains me, Lizzy, you must also think of the practicalities. You are in very grave danger, and there is little your uncle and I can do to protect you beyond what we have already done. In a marriage with Fitzwilliam, you will be protected, and I daresay cherished. You know his father thinks very highly of you; do you think he would not shower you with fatherly care and affection? Really, you are in quite the enviable position. And the match is made. You have no true choice, other than to accept it gracefully or fight like a shrew. Which will it be, my darling niece?"

Regardless of her misgivings, Elizabeth knew there was really no way around it. She must marry Fitzwilliam, and soon, for her own safety and the peace of mind of her family.

"Very well. I will marry him, and I will not fight it. I know that Papa has given Uncle permission to act in his stead, but have you notified him? Will my family come to town for my wedding? I am not certain I wish them to be here."

Elizabeth's thoughts were whirling wildly as her eyes filled with tears.

Shaking, pale, and overcome with emotion, she looked at her companions beseechingly, "Please, forgive me. I find that I need some solitude to reflect upon the situation. May I please go up to my room?"

Mr. Gardiner took pity on her. "Yes, my dear, you may. Rest until supper, and we will call you back down then. If you have any questions, please do not hesitate to ask us. We do not want you to feel alone in this; it is our desire to support you in every way possible."

"Certainly, Uncle. I love you." She hugged him before turning to her aunt to hug her, as well. "I love you, too, Aunt. Thank you both for taking care of me so well."

She walked from the room, their words of love and care ringing in her ears. Upon entering her chambers, Elizabeth threw herself on the bed for a long bout of weeping for what felt to

her like lost dreams, fear of Lord
Regis, and her unknown future.

Chapter 4

Darcy House, London

Two weeks later

Young Fitzwilliam Darcy, age one and twenty and freshly home from his abbreviated Grand Tour, knocked on the door of his father's study. He had wasted little time getting home upon arriving in England. The elder Darcy had sent him an alarming letter while he was in Scotland, and he was anxious to see just what his father was about. Fitzwilliam had great respect for his parent and was in general very obedient. However, to hear that he had been engaged to be married and he knew not to whom …

He prayed fervently the entire trip home that it was not to his cousin, Anne. While he liked her a great deal, he did not wish to marry her. She was quite sickly, and it was not at all certain that she would be able to carry a child safely. As heir to his father's estate, Fitzwilliam knew that having children was an essential part of his duties, and he needed to make sure that whomever he married, she would be healthy enough to birth his heir.

Regardless, the elder Darcy had never promoted a match between him and his cousin. However, he had never specifically spoken against it, either, and Fitzwilliam could not be sure where his father stood on the issue. As much as it would pain him, if George Darcy had betrothed him to Anne, he would have to refuse, no matter the consequences.

Upon hearing his father's bid for him to enter, Fitzwilliam cautiously opened the door and peeked in. "I am home Father; may I come in?"

"Certainly, my boy! It is so good to see you! How was your return trip?" Darcy stood when his son entered, embracing him tightly. It seemed as though he had been gone for years rather than the few months it actually was.

"It was a very comfortable journey. The weather was quite fine, enabling the horses to make excellent time."

"Indeed, that is good to hear! And what of your travels? Did they meet your expectations?"

"Oh, yes, they certainly did! I saw many amazing sights! I daresay I could not have enjoyed myself more had I gone to France and Italy." Fitzwilliam smiled at the memories of the sights he had seen and the adventures he had enjoyed.

"Capital!" responded Mr. Darcy. "I get the impression, though, that you are not here to exclaim over your tour?"

"No, sir, I am not, though I would be more than happy to share tales of my travels with you and Georgiana this evening. For the present, though, I must admit to some consternation regarding your recent letter. Please, tell me you have not promised me to Anne!"

"Anne? No, my son, I know you have no desire to wed your cousin, and I am aware that she shares your opinion. I have instead betrothed you to Elizabeth Bennet." Darcy waited for his son's reaction. He was not entirely sure what it would be.

"Elizabeth Bennet? You cannot be serious." Fitzwilliam was shocked. Never had he expected to hear such a thing come out of his father's mouth. Surely he did not expect his son to marry so far below himself!

"Why can I not be serious? Why not Elizabeth Bennet?" Darcy was biding his time, not giving his son any details just yet. He was well aware that the young man was rather too conscious of the differences between his social class and others. Elizabeth was the daughter of a gentleman, but that gentleman did not move in the same social circles that the Darcys did. He was hoping that Fitzwilliam would not protest too much. He was convinced that the two young people were in love, though not aware of it themselves. He would not move on this. Fitzwilliam would marry Miss Elizabeth, and soon.

"Father … she has an uncle in trade! How is she an appropriate wife for me? Such a marriage would bring scandal to the Darcy name. You cannot have thought this through!" Even as he spoke the words, Fitzwilliam was aware that he was not as shocked as he had been at first. In the back of his mind came the thought, **Why not Miss Elizabeth?** He could not explain the feeling of certainty and peace he felt at the idea, despite his words.

"You are well aware of my friendship with Edward Gardiner. I will not hear words of censure from you regarding his friendship or his relations. I hold the entire family in high regard. If you stop complaining for a moment and think about the relationship between our family and theirs, you will remember that all three of us have professed quite a liking for Miss Elizabeth's company. You certainly have had no cause to repine your association with her. I believe you have quite enjoyed debating her every time the two of you have met." Here Mr. Darcy paused. It was time to lay the facts on the table. He could see that his son's countenance was now more reflective than it had been previously. He was obviously pondering his father's words.

"Elizabeth is in danger. Her mother has been pushing a suitor at her, going so far as to encourage the gentleman to compromise her. This gentleman struck our girl when she refused an offer from him. Mr. Bennet had intuitively known something was amiss, and followed the pair into the garden; he was able to stop the gentleman almost immediately. However, Miss Elizabeth was injured. She was bedbound for a fortnight, during which time her mother harassed her at every turn. Mr. Bennet sent his daughter to London to get her away not only from the man, who is a peer, but from her mother, as well.

"She was here a month when the gentleman showed up at the Gardiners' door, demanding to see her. Gardiner refused, of course. I have hired guards for the outside of the house, and he has moved some strong footmen from his warehouse to his home to keep watch over the residents inside. I fear that Gardiner himself is in danger from this man because of the threats made, as are his wife and children." Darcy paused to gauge his son's reaction before continuing. Fitzwilliam was quiet and pale. Darcy knew his son well enough to know that he was angry. He decided to push a little more.

"You know that you and Miss Elizabeth share many of the same interests. You both enjoy the theater, you share tastes in reading material, and you each enjoy the other's sense of humor. I know you like each other very well. Have you ever noticed how her face lights up when she sees you?"

Here, Fitzwilliam's head came up.

"And Son, yours does the same. You are very well-matched, you and Miss Elizabeth. And to be honest, I have long desired to have her for a daughter. She will make an excellent mistress of Pemberley when I am gone and you take over."

"Father, let us not speak of that! You will be master for many years, I am quite certain." He paused for a moment to examine his feelings and gather his thoughts.

"I am angry that someone would do this to Miss Elizabeth. Who is the man?"

Darcy hesitated. He was unsure of the depth of his son's anger. It would not do for Fitzwilliam to call the gentleman out or in some other way seek retribution.

"I will tell you, but you must promise to not run off and do anything foolish. Do you promise?"

It was Fitzwilliam's turn to hesitate. However, he would always do as his father asked, and once he gave his word, he did not break it. "Yes, Father, I promise."

"The gentleman is Lord Regis." Darcy waited for the reaction.

"But, he is a rake of the worse kind! What is Mrs. Bennet thinking?"

"Mrs. Bennet is thinking about the entail on her husband's estate. She wants to see her daughters well married and taken care of before Mr. Bennet dies. There are many mothers like her in the world, and it would not do to condemn her too harshly. However, you now see the urgency behind my actions?"

"Yes, Father, I do. I will admit, I still have reservations, but I can certainly see that marriage to me would enable us to protect Miss Elizabeth. At the same time, it will ease her mother's concerns. I cannot believe, though, that she took the news with equanimity. Have you heard from Mr. Gardiner in regards to it?"

"As a matter of fact, Gardiner and I had luncheon together yesterday, as we had business to discuss. I believe Miss Elizabeth took the news about as well as you did. However, she has had a great fright and recognizes the advantages in regards to the safety of herself and her family. She has agreed to the marriage. You know, though, that ladies like to be asked by the gentleman they will marry. Perhaps we should make the trip to Gracechurch Street today, and you can begin on the right foot. I am sure that under the circumstances you will be allowed a few minutes of private time with her." Darcy rose to ring the bell.

"Yes, I am sure you are right. Let us go now. Perhaps we might invite the family to dine with us this evening?"

"Certainly, Son." Darcy was quite pleased. He thought the interview went very well, indeed.

~~~***~~~

Once at the Gardner residence, Darcy and his son were shown into the family parlor. There, Maddie, Elizabeth, Edward, and the children were gathered. Elizabeth was playing with the youngsters, while Maddie looked on with a fond smile and Gardiner perused his newspaper, calling out occasional comments and teases to the little ones.

Mr. Gibson, the Gardiners' butler, announced the visitors. "Mr. Darcy and Mr. Fitzwilliam Darcy."

After greetings were shared and everyone was seated, Gardiner asked his friend, "What brings you to visit this fine afternoon?" He suspected the reason, based on the looks being bestowed upon Elizabeth by Fitzwilliam.

Darcy replied, "Well, Gardiner, my son and I had a long discussion today, and
~~~

it seems he would like some time to chat with Miss Elizabeth."

Lizzy blushed to the roots of her hair. She knew exactly what the **chat** would involve. She was still uncomfortable with the idea of marrying a gentleman she was not sure she loved, but she understood both the necessity and the advantages of it.

Fitzwilliam also blushed. While his father had assured him of Miss Elizabeth's cooperation, he was still uncomfortable with the idea of marrying someone not only not of his circle in society, but also someone of whose feelings toward him he was unsure. However, he came here to ask her to marry him, and ask he would.

"Yes, Father, Mr. Gardiner, I would like a few minutes to talk to Miss Elizabeth, in private, if I may?"

"You may, Fitzwilliam. Why do your father and I not retreat to my study?"

Mrs. Gardiner rose as the gentlemen did. "I believe I will take my children back to their nanny now. It will soon be time for supper, and they must be made ready." She took her offspring, one by the hand and one in her arms, and led them upstairs while the older gentlemen left for Gardiner's study.

When they were alone, Elizabeth sat down, folding her hands in her lap. She was suddenly overcome with shyness, an unusual occurrence. Fitzwilliam paced the parlor for a few minutes before stopping in front of her and gently clearing his throat.

"Miss Elizabeth …" Here he paused. Was this how a young lady would wish to receive a proposal? He wished he had thought to bring her flowers, but neither he nor his father had contemplated it and it was too late now. He would have to do without. Suddenly, it occurred to him to get down on one knee. Accordingly, he knelt in front of

Elizabeth and took one of her hands in his own.

"Miss Elizabeth, my father explained your circumstances to me, and that he and your uncle have engaged us to be married. I know I do not need to, but I would like for us to proceed as though our attachment was not arranged, and I know ladies appreciate romance. I also know we do not love each other at this time. I have faith, though, that our feelings for each other will grow. We are alike in many ways, and I believe we are compatible. You are an intelligent woman, and I foresee you someday becoming the greatest mistress that Pemberley has ever had.

"In addition, I know you are in danger from Lord Regis. Our betrothal and marriage will protect you from him; I will make sure of that." As Fitzwilliam spoke, that sense of peace he had felt deep inside as he had spoken with his father about his marriage returned and intensified. Somehow, he knew this was the correct path for them to be taking. It was as though they had always been meant for each other. He could imagine asking no other to share his life.

"Would you do me the great honor of becoming my wife?"

As Fitzwilliam spoke, Elizabeth was feeling the same sense of tranquility, despite her misgivings. She knew he had reservations about the marriage, as well, but he had agreed to both keep her safe and honor his father's wishes.

"Yes, Fitzwilliam, I will marry you." No words had ever sounded sweeter to either of them.

"Thank you, Elizabeth." Fitzwilliam dug into his waistcoat pocket. "I brought this for you. It was my mother's, and I know she would want me to give it to my betrothed."

He slid the ring, a beautiful gold band studded with diamonds and emeralds, onto her finger, then kissed it.

"I promise to be the best husband I can be for you. I will always respect and honor you."

"Thank you, Fitzwilliam. I make a promise to you, as well, that I will be the best wife and mistress of your future homes that I can be, and I will always show you the same honor and respect."

Chapter 5

Gardiner House, London

One week later

The household on Gracechurch Street was quiet, the last of the residents finally settling in to sleep. The footmen on duty during the night listened carefully for the snores and sighs that indicated all was well before settling into their positions.

Suddenly, the man posted upstairs stiffened. He had heard something, a sound that did not belong. He held his breath, alert for it to come again. He did not have long to wait. Creeping down the hallway as quietly as possible, he stopped outside the room beside Miss Elizabeth's, putting his hand on the latch. From the other side of the door, he heard a muffled oath.

The footman flung the wooden panel open and rushed into the room, in time to catch sight of a man running for the open window. He threw himself at the intruder in an effort to bring him to the floor. The man was too quick, however, and escaped out the window. The footman watched as the man ran through the back garden and into the alley that ran beside the house, the guard from outside close on his heels.

"Cooper, what is going on?" Mr. Gardiner stood in the doorway of the guest room, candle in hand, in his nightshirt.

"We had an intruder, sir. I heard him moving around in here, but he was too quick for me to catch. I am sorry. Johnson is hard after him, though. I wish I had been a little faster." Cooper frowned.

By this time, more of the household had arisen, including Mrs. Gardiner and Elizabeth. Both appeared frightened, and Lizzy was hanging on to Maddie. Mr. Gardiner began making requests.

"Gibson, please have someone light the candles in this room, and bring more up. We need to check that nothing has been disturbed, though I do not believe this was a robbery attempt. I think we all know who it was that came through the window and what his purpose was." At this, Elizabeth and Mrs. Gardiner gasped, holding each other more tightly.

"Yes, sir," the butler responded, signalling to a maid to gather more candles as he went about the room lighting the ones that were there. Once there was enough light, it was plain to see that nothing had been disturbed except the counterpane on the bed. That item was pulled down, as though someone was going to get under it on the bed, and the sheet below was mussed.

Mr. Gardiner sighed. His worst fears were being realized.

"My dears," he said to his wife and niece, "it appears that Lord Regis has struck. I believe that he was attempting to harm Lizzy, either through kidnapping or a compromise." What Mr. Gardiner did not say, and hoped his niece, at least, did not realize, was the likely extent of Regis' actions if he had managed to get to Elizabeth.

Elizabeth turned her face into her aunt's shoulder and began sobbing. She was terrified at the thought that the gentleman would try to do this. She did not feel safe, and this made her feel guilty. Why did he not just give her up? Why alarm her in this manner? And how was she to tell her beloved aunt and uncle that she did not feel safe in their house?

"Gibson, we should get my study ready for visitors, as I believe Johnson will soon return to report to me."

"Very good, sir." The butler turned to go, shooing the rest of the servants out ahead of him.

To his wife and niece, Gardiner said, "Let us wait for Johnson to return, and see what he has to say. Perhaps he has caught the man, and it was not who we think it is." Even as the words formed in his mouth, Gardiner knew in his heart they were false. Elizabeth and Mrs. Gardiner believed the same, though they kept their thoughts to themselves.

The three moved down the stairs and into the study. Gibson and a maid soon appeared with a tea tray.

"I thought some refreshments might be helpful while you wait."

"Thank you, Gibson, that will be all. Please have the maids retire. There is no need for us all to be up."

"As you wish, sir." With that, Gibson removed himself from the room to his office. He knew he would be needed again this night, if for nothing more than to admit Johnson.

After Gibson left the study, Gardiner reflected on the events of the night, and how his staff and Darcy's had reacted to them. As the highest ranking staff members, both Gibson and the housekeeper were aware of the true situation with Miss Elizabeth and her persistent suitor. The lower staff had been told that the new footmen were just that—footmen—and did not know that they were, in fact, guarding the family.

Mr. Gardiner knew Gibson's heart ached for Miss Elizabeth. Both she and her sister Jane were great favorites of his staff. The girls were unfailingly polite to everyone, regardless of rank or position. He also knew the staff's opinion about the rest of his family; they were demanding and oft-times rude, and his brother Bennet frequently gave people the impression he was laughing at them all.

~~~***~~~

In the study, Elizabeth and her family were discussing the night's events. Lizzy was quite shaken, her aunt and uncle only a little less so.

"Do you think he will come back, Uncle Edward?" Elizabeth's voice trembled. Her arms were wrapped around her middle and she rocked slightly back and forth, as if to comfort herself. Maddie sat in the chair next to her, with her arm around Lizzy's shoulders.
~~~

"We have no way of knowing, my dear. I would like to think he would realize we are in a state of heightened alert, but any man crazy enough to break into a house cannot be trusted to stay away once he has been discovered." Gardiner hated to increase her fear, but he knew Elizabeth would want the bare facts. She was an intelligent and independent young lady who would resent being treated like a child, no matter how ill at ease she was currently feeling.

As Gardiner finished speaking, the trio heard a knock on the study door. Upon being bid entrance, Gibson opened the panel to announce the guard, Avery Johnson. Johnson was one of the large, burly, but nimble men Darcy had hired to guard the house. Darcy had explained some of Johnson's history to him, and after meeting the man, Gardiner had come away with a large amount of respect for the young fellow, whose roots were deep in the worst part of the city.

Gardiner immediately got down to business. "Johnson, what news have you of our intruder?"

"Aye was not able to catch 'im, sir, but aye can tell you what aye seen of 'im, if ye like."

"Indeed, please do."

"'E 'ad fine clothes on, no' like what aye'd wear, but like ye might, or Mist'r Darcy would. He must 'ave 'ad a carriage waitin' fer 'im. 'E jumped inta one a few streets away. It 'ad no markin's on it; plain it was."

"Were you able to see his face?" Lizzy asked the question that all three wanted to know.

"No'm, aye dinna see 'is face, but aye did follo' 'im 'ome, as it were. 'E 'eaded inta Mayfair, stoppin' a' a house on Belgrave, nummer six."

At this, the Gardiners and Elizabeth looked at each other. They had their proof. The man who entered their house illicitly was none other than Lord Regis.

"Thank you, Johnson; my family and I appreciate the effort you made to catch this man. There will be a bonus in your pay this week, I am sure. Please take a few hours off and get some rest. I will send for one of the other men to cover for you."

Johnson bowed and with a "Thankee sir," he left the room.

"What are we to do, Uncle," cried Elizabeth, her voice rising as her anxiety grew. "How are we to rest knowing he is out there?"

Maddie spoke up. "Edward, it is apparent to me that Lizzy cannot stay here. Is it possible to take her to Darcy House? I know it is late and the Darcys are likely sleeping, but would they not want to know what has happened? I know they would be willing to at least let Lizzy stay the night."

Gardiner thought for a few moments, staring into the candle flame as he tried to order his thoughts. "I believe you are correct, my dear. Lizzy, what say you. Will you feel safer at Darcy House?"

Immediately Elizabeth agreed. "I do not wish to hurt the two of you, as I know you have done everything you could to keep me safe, but I would indeed feel better at Darcy House. Please, may we go?"

"Let me ring for the carriage; we will leave as soon as we are dressed." Gardiner rang the bell, and when Gibson attended him, asked that the carriage be readied. "We will go out through the kitchen, so have the coachman keep it waiting back there."

As Gibson left the room, followed by Elizabeth, Maddie, and Gardiner, the master of the house prayed that they would get to Darcy House safely, that Lizzy would finally be safe, and that Lord Regis would at last let her go.

Chapter 6

Darcy House, London

3 AM

Darcy House was quiet, its residents tucked up in their beds, when there came a ferocious banging on the door to the servants' entrance. Mr. Baxter, the butler, roused a footman to accompany him, and then approached the door.

"Who's there?" He called through the wooden panel.

The response came. "Edward Gardiner. I have my niece with me and urgently need to see Mr. Darcy."

Mr. Baxter had been alerted by his employer that Mr. Gardiner was always to be granted entrance, so the butler cautiously opened the panel.

Once he was sure the visitor was truly the master's friend, he threw the door back and hurried the gentleman and his niece into the house. He was shocked to see that Miss Bennet appeared distraught and wondered what could have happened.

"Please, I know it is very late, but I need to speak to Mr. Darcy immediately. It is a matter of dire importance."

"Of course, sir." Mr. Baxter turned to the footman. "Wake Reeves and have him bring the master to the kitchen." To Gardiner he said, "There is no fire in the drawing room. You will be more comfortable here in the kitchen. Miss Bennet, allow me to pull out one of these stools; please rest while you await Mr. Darcy."

"Thank you, sir." Miss Bennet's voice was soft, but Mr. Baxter could detect a note of fear in it. This greatly concerned him. Miss Bennet was a great favorite with all the servants at Darcy House and he did not like seeing her in distress. She was usually so cheerful and happy. He wondered what had happened. He vowed to himself that if necessary, he would avenge her, and he knew the footmen and stable boys would back him up.

Soon, Mr. Darcy rushed into the kitchen, closely followed by his son. Elizabeth and her uncle quickly stood, Elizabeth with a definite wobble. Fitzwilliam rushed to her side, putting his arm around her and helping her to sit back down on the stool. He could see that she was upset and all of his protective instincts came to the fore.

"Gardiner, what is the matter? What has happened?" Darcy sounded slightly out of breath; he had rushed to the kitchen as soon as summoned. He knew his friend would not have come knocking in the middle of the night, at the servants' entrance, for no reason.

He had been quite alarmed when his valet awakened him with the news.

"Lord Regis has made an attempt to get to Elizabeth." Everyone in the room knew who he was talking about, so Gardner felt no need to explain. More than that, he did not want to frighten his niece any more than she already was. With their quick and clever minds, he was sure the Darcy gentlemen would figure out the truth without further details.

"He tried to break into a bedroom through a window. I believe he thought it was Lizzy's, but it was a guest room. I am thankful I took you up on your offer of protection and that you hired men to guard the place at night. The sentry posted outside saw the ladder at about the same time as the one in the upstairs hall heard a noise. The intruder got away, but the guard followed him to a house here in Mayfair. It was definitely Lord Regis.

The commotion woke the entire household. My wife and I no longer feel that we can keep Lizzy safe ..."

At this, Fitzwilliam interrupted. He could see the strain in Elizabeth's eyes and knew she needed rest. At the same time, he knew how he could keep her safe. He had, with his father's and Gardner's permission, already bought a special license. He could marry Lizzy at any time and in any place. The marriage articles had already been signed. There was nothing standing in their way. He would marry her now, as soon as the bishop got here, and Elizabeth would be protected, as he and his father would make sure Lord Regis would be unable to get close enough to her to cause problems. Picking her up off the stool, he strode to the door to the hallway.

"Father, send for my uncle, the bishop. I am taking Elizabeth to our room." Fitzwilliam and Elizabeth had briefly discussed their post-marital sleeping arrangements, but had made no firm decision. With Georgiana still in the nursery, there was the space for them to each have their own room, though that is not what Fitzwilliam wanted. Elizabeth had not insisted on it, either. He did not want to make assumptions; however, at this moment in time it mattered not to Fitzwilliam what their future plans may or may not be. She needed to rest, and he needed to make that happen. He was not about to take additional time to rouse someone to prepare an extra room, thereby delaying Lizzy's comfort.

Neither Darcy nor Gardiner batted an eyelash. It had been obvious for the past week that the two young people had not only reconciled themselves to their arranged marriage, they were well on their way to falling deeply in love. They would allow Fitzwilliam to do what he felt he must.

~~~***~~~

Fitzwilliam climbed quickly up the servant's stairs to the floor where the family's quarters were. He could feel Elizabeth's arms around him, hands clutching his shoulder and one side of his neck, with her face buried in the other side. He whispered words of comfort to her, dropping occasional kisses into her hair. Soon they had arrived at his chambers. He struggled a bit with the latch, but quickly made his way inside, depositing his lovely burden on the bed. Elizabeth sat quietly where he had set her, tears running down her face. Fitzwilliam's heart contracted to see her so distressed. He sat beside her and wrapped her in his embrace.

"Let me take care of you," he whispered as he held her. She nodded against his shoulder, and Fitzwilliam began to unfasten the morning dress she was wearing. He eased it down to
~~~

her waist and then stood her up to push it and her petticoat down to the floor. After laying her on the bed, he removed her slippers along with his own boots and tailcoat. He had gotten dressed too quickly to worry about a waistcoat when he had been awakened upon Lizzy's arrival. Finally, he lay down beside her, cradling his betrothed in his arms and covering the two of them with a quilt. She felt so right there. He suddenly realized just **how** undressed she was. Certainly she was still in her corset, chemise, and stockings, but to be so close to her when she was in her undergarments made his pulse pound. However, she was still weeping silent tears. Any even remotely lascivious thoughts were thrust to the back of his mind as he held her tight and attempted to soothe her.

Fitzwilliam whispered more words of care and comfort and love to her as she began falling asleep. **Yes – love**, he thought. **I love her. I do not know how it happened, but she has captured my heart.** He was most pleased by the realization.

As he thought further, imagining telling her what was in his heart, Fitzwilliam paused. He was well aware that Elizabeth did not love him, at least not yet. If he shared his feelings with her, she might feel bound to say the words back to him regardless of her own feelings. At the very least she would be made uncomfortable, and that would not do. He could not add to the anxiety she was already feeling. No, he would keep his sentiments to himself but would continue to court her even after the wedding. In his heart, he was assured that one day his Elizabeth would love him back; at that time he would feel free to speak those words to her. His last thoughts as he drifted off to sleep were happy plans for their life together.

~~~***~~~

A couple hours later, William's valet, Smith, quietly spoke to him. "Sir ... sir ... your father requests your presence and that of the young lady in the blue parlor. The bishop is here."

"Thank you, Smith," Fitzwilliam whispered, looking over his shoulder at the gentleman.

He looked back to Lizzy, who was softly snoring in his arms. He hated to wake her. She had been so upset when he brought her upstairs that he was hesitant to distress her again. However, they needed to get married, and his uncle was here to perform the ceremony.

"Lizzy," he whispered into her hair. "Come, my love, we must rise and greet the bishop. It is our wedding day."
~~~

Lizzy startled at his soft voice and the kiss he bestowed on her ear. For a brief second she was confused, before the events of the previous night flooded her memory. She tensed, causing Fitzwilliam to gently squeeze her.

"All will be well, Elizabeth. Trust me. We will marry, and once you are officially a Darcy, Lord Regis will no longer be a threat to you. We have the standing and resources to stand up to him. You will be safe."

Lizzy nodded, relaxing a bit in his arms. She did feel safer here at Darcy House than she had at her uncle's. She was surprised she got any sleep at all, but even last night in the middle of her crisis, when Fitzwilliam picked her up to carry her upstairs, it had felt as though she had always been there. She almost felt like she had come home. She would have liked to ponder these thoughts and feelings for a while, but Fitzwilliam was insistent that she get up and dress.

Abruptly, Lizzy realized that she was wearing nothing but her undergarments and blushed profusely. She had vague memories of Fitzwilliam removing her dress. She was exceedingly embarrassed to be seen by her betrothed in such a state, and the fact that he was the reason she was undressed to begin with made it worse. She could not look him in the face as he gently helped her into her gown and fastened it up.

Fitzwilliam's feelings, on the other hand, were harder to define. He was very much aware of the impropriety of bringing her to his room, then essentially stripping her before sleeping with her. Never mind that they did just that—sleep. Despite the slightly guilty feelings he had in regards to those actions, he was very happy to serve his wife—for that is how he thought of her and indeed she was very nearly—in such a gentle manner. Thoughts of what would happen the next time he helped her out of her dress were trying very hard to take over his mind, but he valiantly fought them. Now was not the time or place.

After affixing the last button, Fitzwilliam turned his attention to Elizabeth's countenance. She would not look at him, and he could see that the tips of her ears were red. He tilted her face up to his with his finger under her chin. Soon she was forced to look into his eyes and see their expression.

Elizabeth's mortification was eased by the affection and warmth she saw there. As she began to smile at him, her betrothed leaned in and softly touched his lips to hers in their first shared kiss.

"Now, my beautiful girl, are you ready to be married?"

"Yes, Fitzwilliam, I am, but I believe there may be something wrong with your eyes, for we both know I am not beautiful," she said with a smile and a lifted eyebrow.

Fitzwilliam broke into a grin. She was teasing him! It eased his worries about the state of her emotions. "Indeed, I do not. You are certainly the most beautiful lady I have ever laid eyes upon. Your sister Jane is nothing to you, I assure you, and I insist that you allow me to tell you. You must, you know, as you are about to vow to obey me for the remainder of our lives."

At this, Elizabeth giggled. It felt good to tease and be teased and forget for a few minutes the pain and tension that had filled her life these past few months.

The couple stared at each other for a brief time, smiling widely, before Smith once again stuck his head in the door and cleared his throat. Suddenly, the smiles were wiped off their faces as the seriousness of their situation and what they were about to do struck them. Holding hands, they left the room and descended the staircase, ready to begin the ceremony that would join them forever.

Chapter 7

Although there had not been time to plan a wedding breakfast for the couple, the cook, who had arisen about the time the bishop arrived, had managed to produce a meal for the assembled company to share. Accordingly, the bride and groom, the groom's father, the bride's aunt, uncle, and cousins, and the clergyman all made their way to the breakfast room to celebrate.

Elizabeth's aunt and the children had arrived shortly before the bishop. Gardiner had not felt comfortable leaving them at home and, in his mind, unprotected; Mr. Darcy concurred and sent footmen and his own carriage to the Gardiner house to transport them to Darcy House. The family would stay at the Darcy home for a few days, until other arrangements could be made or until the gentlemen felt sure that the threat from Lord Regis was eliminated. Elizabeth was thrilled to see her entire London family in the Darcys' parlor when she walked in for the ceremony. Having them in attendance made it all seem so much more real.

During the meal, the gentlemen discussed their next steps. Darcy had already written out an announcement to send to the papers. He had sent a boy out to deliver it as soon as the newspaper offices opened. Hopefully, the evening editions would print it today, and the Morning Post would have it in tomorrow's edition. In the meantime, he and Gardiner would spread the news to the gentlemen they knew to be in contact with Lord Regis. Their stated hope was that the gentleman would immediately stop his harassment of Elizabeth; their unstated worry was that he would not.

It had been decided immediately upon Elizabeth accepting Fitzwilliam's hand that the two would marry at Darcy House and, directly after the wedding breakfast, retire upstairs to a suite of rooms, as far away from the crowd of family and visitors as possible, to enjoy a week of honeymooning. In reality, it was a small suite, just a sitting room, bedroom, and dressing room that they would have to share; but they would have the space to themselves and would not need to leave the chambers for any reason unless they chose to. Smith had spent part of a day moving things from Fitzwilliam's room to this one in preparation for this time. By the end of the honeymoon period, the young couple would decide they liked the suite enough that it became theirs permanently, until the time came for Fitzwilliam to become master.

The reasoning behind the speed of their retirement to this suite of rooms was to make the union official in all ways, thereby reducing any attempts—or even the desire to attempt—to dissolve it. There was not only Lord Regis to think about in this matter. There was also Fitzwilliam's maternal aunt, Lady Catherine de Bourgh, his mother's sister, who had claimed the young man for her daughter for years. She would be made unhappy by his marriage, and every effort must be made by the couple and their families to solidify the union in everyone's mind before that lady could interrupt it. While the marriage could not be annulled because it was unconsummated, Darcy would not put it past his sister to make the attempt.

Debate had raged for several hours on the topic of a honeymoon tour of some sort, but in the end, it was decided that going away from Darcy House increased the risk to Elizabeth. No one knew how Lord Regis would react to the wedding announcement, and none wanted to take the chance of being caught out with less than ex-cellent protection.

Therefore, after eating breakfast, the gentlemen removed themselves to Darcy's study, while Mrs. Gardiner and Georgiana moved to the music room. This left the new couple alone in the breakfast room, blushes on their faces.

"Well, Wife, shall we go upstairs and inspect our new rooms?" Fitzwilliam rose and held out his hand to his wife. **Wife**, he thought, smiling to himself, **how well that sounds!**

Lizzy put her hand in his and gracefully rose. The couple slowly left the room and ascended the stairs. Both were consumed with their own thoughts, which were rather similar. Both were nervous about what was to come and embarrassed that others were in the house and would know what they were doing. Both did feel more at ease knowing that they would be doing this as far from their family members as it was possible to be while all remained crowded into one house.

Fitzwilliam's nervousness quickly eased, however. Those thoughts that had entered his mind while he helped Lizzy dress a couple hours ago rushed back full force, causing a distinct reaction in his person. Concerned that he would frighten Lizzy, he took a few deep breaths and thought about his Aunt Catherine. **There. That would keep him on an even keel for a while.**

Elizabeth's thoughts about what was to come were confused. Her aunt had spoken with her a few days prior about what to expect, but there were so many uncertainties. So many details of which she was unsure, that her aunt had left out. Rather than work herself up into a fit of nerves, Lizzy took a few deep breaths and turned to look at her new husband as they entered their suite of rooms. They had promised each other respect, and she knew Fitzwilliam's character enough to trust he would neither hurt her nor demand things from her that she was unable to give. He would be gentle with her, she knew.

Later that day ...

Elizabeth woke a few hours later, head pillowed on Fitzwilliam's shoulder, knee thrown over his thigh. He was tightly wrapped around her, an arm around her shoulder, the other hand wrapped around her waist. She lay quietly so as not to disturb his rest, and reflected on her experiences of the last week.

~~~***~~~

The day of his proposal, Fitzwilliam and his father invited Lizzy and her London family to Darcy House to dine. The thought of leaving the house so
~~~

late in the afternoon caused her no small amount of anxiety, an emotion she thought she had hidden well. Fitzwilliam saw it, however, and made every effort to put her at ease. He remained by her side as much as possible, speaking quietly to her in an effort to put her at ease and distract her. His attentiveness was heart-warming, which gave Elizabeth a sense of relief and hope. Perhaps their marriage would indeed turn out well.

For the next week, Fitzwilliam was at the Gardiner house as often as possible. The couple took many long walks in the park near the Gardiner's home, chaperoned by a maid. They had always enjoyed debating, and during these walks, they continued that pastime. He brought her flowers every day, accompanied by small gifts. Some of these gifts were little things he picked up while out on business with his father. A slim volume of poetry written by Lizzy's favorite author one day, a dainty carved box to hold hairpins the next, a box of dried plums the day after that. Some days Fitzwilliam brought her gifts of jewels and other items that his mother had left him to give to his wife. No matter the gift, they were always thoughtfully given and greatly appreciated. It was obvious to Lizzy that the gentleman had observed her well and was eager to please her.

The theater trip planned by her aunt and uncle had expanded to include the Darcys, and moved from general seating on the floor to the Darcys' box seats. Fitzwilliam had told her, as they walked into the theater that night, how proud he was to attend with the most gorgeous lady in London, at least in his opinion, on his arm.

Dressed in a gown of the deepest forest green, Elizabeth was stunning. Her continued apprehension regarding

Lord Regis kept her eyes lowered, giving her an appearance of shyness, and Fitzwilliam's frequent compliments caused her to blush almost constantly, adding color to her otherwise pale complexion.

This night at the theater went a long way to helping Elizabeth recognize that she had feelings for the gentleman she would soon call her husband.

By the time the Gardiners and Darcys arrived at the theater, there was a crush of people spilling out the doors. Fitzwilliam was visibly ill at ease, as he always was in large crowds, but Elizabeth could see that he was determined to push his disquiet aside to help her deal with hers.

His father disembarked the carriage first, with Fitzwilliam following. The latter walked back to the Gardiners' carriage in time to assist his soon-to-be wife. He wrapped her hand around his arm, and placed his free hand over hers. Speaking quietly to her, he asked, "Well, my sweet, are you ready to face the **ton**?"

Elizabeth gave him a small smile. "Yes, Fitzwilliam, I am as ready as I will ever be. Surely they cannot be any more frightening than Lord Regis; quite possibly less so."

Fitzwilliam had laughed, "Indeed you are correct, Elizabeth. Let us go inside, then."

The two followed the Gardiners and Fitzwilliam's family into the building. The noise of conversation inside lowered as Fitzwilliam and Elizabeth entered before rising again as the theater-goers tried to figure out who the young lady was who clung to Fitzwilliam Darcy's arm. The attention was unnerving for the previously impervious Elizabeth, and the hand she had around her betrothed's arm unconsciously tightened its grip. Fitzwilliam, whose free hand still covered hers, squeezed it a bit before leaning down to whisper to her, "Courage, my dear. Their weapons are words; they are nothing to a lady as witty as you. I and the rest of your family will remain near. These people cannot touch you."

Elizabeth smiled up at him, whispering, "Thank you, Husband."

Fitzwilliam gave her a brilliant smile in return, causing a gasp to arise among the many in the crowd who were observing. Mr. Darcy the younger was not known to smile. His reputation amongst the **ton** was that of a serious, dour gentleman not given to carousing or gossip. That the mystery lady was able to draw a smile out of him was astounding, and many of the young ladies present wished it was they on his arm. Speculation and rumors about Elizabeth's identity grew wildly, continuing even after the two families had left the lobby and entered their box.

Upon entering the box, the various family members arranged themselves in the chairs. Darcy and Gardiner sat together, with Georgiana and Maddie in front of them. Elizabeth and Fitzwilliam sat to the left of the ladies, beside each other. Fitzwilliam had explained to her that he was determined to be near her at all times this night, for several reasons. For one, he knew she was uneasy; for two, he knew she did not wish to confront Lord Regis, should he be in attendance. In addition to these explanations, Lizzy was aware that he was doing his best to court her.

Soon enough, the play began. Fitzwilliam's right hand crept over to Elizabeth's, which was resting on the bench between them. Though she was startled, she gave no indication that she disliked holding his hand. In fact, she turned hers over and their fingers entwined under the edge of her skirt.

Holding her future husband's hand was very comforting to Elizabeth. She enjoyed it very much, actually. She was happy he had taken the initiative the way he had. She knew it was against propriety to touch in such a manner, especially in public, but she did not care. No one could see them, and she thought it was quite delightful. In fact, it led her to wonder what other liberties Fitzwilliam might attempt to take and how she would feel about it if he did. She had to admit that she wondered what it would be like to kiss him.

She really had little notion of what went on in the marriage bed. Her aunt had spoken to her about it just today, as Lizzy was away from her own mother and was getting married so quickly; however, she had really not spoken of the specifics of the act, only saying that there would be disrobing and touching occurring and to relax and follow her husband's lead. As a result, Lizzy's imagination was all that she had to go on. But, thinking about liberties made her blush brightly, and she did not want to spend her entire betrothal, nor even this entire night, blushing, so she decided she had best think of other things.

Too soon the play ended, and they had to revert to strictly proper behavior. Lord Regis had not been in attendance, and while many people had stopped them on the way out of the building, trying to gain an introduction to Elizabeth and some tidbit of gossip to spread, both families left for home pleased with the evening.

~~~***~~~

All these thoughts ran through Elizabeth's head on the first day of her marriage, as she lay quietly in her new
~~~

husband's arms. She had always been a person who required time alone to contemplate things, so she was taking advantage of this time to examine Fitzwilliam's actions during their brief courtship. He had shown himself to be a very thoughtful, sensitive gentleman. Elizabeth knew her feelings for him were growing. She was not sure that she loved him, but she certainly cared deeply for him. She knew that her natural ease with people had changed since Lord Regis assaulted her. She was not as easy with others, especially new acquaintances. With Fitzwilliam she felt like she was able to leave that behind, feeling and acting more like herself. For the first time in weeks—months, even—she felt hopeful. Perhaps this marriage and her life would be happy after all.

~~~***~~~
~~~

A couple days later, the couple finally emerged from their rooms. They arrived at breakfast, late, holding hands. The Gardiners and Darcy laughed heartily at the satisfied smile on Fitzwilliam's face and the downcast eyes and blushing countenance of Elizabeth. Thankfully for the new couple, laugh is all they did. There was too much to discuss to spend much time tormenting them this morning.

Sitting on the table between Elizabeth's place and Fitzwilliam's was a folded-up newssheet. Fitzwilliam sat Lizzy down, and then went to the sideboard to make her up a plate. Lizzy picked up the paper and noted the circled item. It was a notice of their marriage, printed in the previous day's newspaper. "Fitzwilliam, look," she remarked when he sat down beside her. She handed the paper to her husband, pointing out the notice.

He took the sheet, smiling happily. The world, including Lord Regis, now knew that Elizabeth was his. He was under no misapprehension that the gentleman would quietly turn his attention elsewhere, however. Fitzwilliam was quite sure Regis would not go away quietly.

"Father," he began, "what are your thoughts about Lord Regis? While I would hope he would simply give Elizabeth up, I do not want to make assumptions. His behavior towards her has been indicative of a gentleman who fully intends possession. I fear our marriage might only slow him down, rather than stop him."

George Darcy nodded as he swallowed his bite of breakfast. "Indeed, my thoughts were similar. To that end, I have hired a gentleman to follow him. Gardiner and I discussed the matter the morning of your wedding, as we waited for your godfather to arrive, and came to the conclusion that we need to remain aware of Lord Regis' movements in order to keep Elizabeth safe. The gentleman has become more aggressive—unpredictable, even—since he has returned to town. Your wedding announcement, as you have seen," he gestured to the paper that was once again lying on the table between Fitzwilliam's plate and Elizabeth's, "was in yesterday morning's Post. I am sure Regis will have seen it by this morning, and his reaction will tell us much. I fully expect a report from the investigator in the next day or two."

Gardiner spoke up next. "Yes, and once we are aware of his reaction to your marriage, my wife and I will be able to decide our next move, as well. As much as all of us have enjoyed being here at Darcy House, it is not our home. We would like to pick our lives back up. Lizzy, this does not mean we are no longer concerned for you; we are. However, you now have a husband and father-in-law to assure your safety. We do not want to upset you, but we and our children need to resume our lives in a normal fashion."

He hesitated, trying to read Lizzy's expression. He did not want to distress her, especially knowing as he did that she had been emotionally fragile for months, but she was no longer his responsibility. He had done his best by her, and her condition was now the purview of her spouse and his father. "Do you understand, my dear?" he asked gently.

Lizzy was quiet for a moment, looking down at her empty plate. "Yes, Uncle," she responded softly. "I do understand, and I agree that you and Aunt Maddie and the children need to move back to Gracechurch Street. I will be well. Fitzwilliam and Mr. Darcy will make sure of it." She gave her uncle a wavering smile. Truly, she did understand.

"I appreciate everything you have done for me, Uncle Edward, Aunt Maddie. I cannot begin to imagine where I would be had you not allowed me to stay with you, and arranged my marriage. Thank you."

Fitzwilliam reached under the table for her hand, giving it a squeeze. Her Aunt Maddie, who was sitting on Lizzy's other side, leaned over to squeeze the other one. For the first time in quite a while, she felt her courage rise. She squeezed the hands that held hers and lifted her chin. She knew there may still be danger in her future from her rejected suitor, but she had support from her family, both her new family and the one she had been a part of her entire life. "I will be fine here. I am well-protected and unafraid."

Bravely, Lizzy smiled at each person around the table. While they knew she did not feel as secure as she let on, they also knew she had made the decision to move on. She would be well, and they were more at ease with their decision to go home.

Soon after, the family members separated, Darcy to his study and his correspondence, Maddie to the nursery to spend time with her children and Georgiana, Gardiner to his warehouse, and the newlyweds upstairs to continue their honeymoon.

The same day, in another part of London ...

Harold Watson, Lord Regis, was in a terrible mood. His attempt to remove the lady he wanted from her relatives' home had not only failed, he was almost caught in the attempt. He had come to his club today, looking for a game of cards and a drink to relieve some of his tension. He continued to be astounded and confounded by that unappreciative chit Elizabeth's ungratefulness for all he offered her. Who else would want a poor, unconnected country girl? She **would** be his, sooner rather than later.

As he had arrived at the club too early for a card game, he sat down with a copy of the paper, accepting a glass of port from the servant on duty. Opening the newssheet, he spent some time reading the war reports and other serious news before skimming the society pages and announcements. Suddenly he choked, spewing the mouthful of port he had just swilled all over himself, the table, and the newspaper. He quickly shook the droplets of wine off the paper as the servant tried to sop up the mess. **There it was**, he thought to himself as he caught sight of the announcement that had so startled him.

In the section for wedding announcements, he read: **Fitzwilliam Darcy, son of Mr. George Darcy, Pemberley, Derbyshire and Brook Street, London to Miss Elizabeth Bennet, daughter of Mr. Thomas Bennet, Longbourn, Hertfordshire.**

Lord Regis read the announcement again, and then a third time. Each time his eyes passed over the words, his rage grew. **No!** he thought, **she belongs to me!** He unexpectedly stood, shoving the hapless footman out of his way as he strode toward the exit. Other members of the club scurried out of his way; they knew by the look on his face that to do otherwise could turn out very badly.

As he reached the sidewalk in front of the club, Regis knew that as much as he wanted to go to Darcy House and resolve the situation, he needed to have a plan in place. To confront George Darcy without one was foolish. However, his rage was such that he was unable to think clearly. He needed to release some energy. He contemplated his options, at first thinking to head to Angelo's and find someone with whom he could fence. But no, fencing was too refined. He required an extremely physical activity that required more brawn than finesse. **Boxing would do**, he thought; accordingly, he moved in the direction of his favorite pugilist's club.

Two hours and four opponents later, Lord Regis was still angry; far too angry to confront the Darcys. What he would like would be to beat Elizabeth into submission, and revenge himself for her betrayal. Since he could not reach Elizabeth at the moment, he looked for a substitute. Elizabeth would get hers, sooner or later. Until then, he would have to make do.

Chapter 8

Darcy House, London

Four days after the wedding

Darcy House was quiet this morning. Mrs. Gardiner and her children were upstairs in the nursery spending time together. Mr. Gardiner had left early in the morning for a business meeting in his office, and George Darcy had an appointment on Bond Street with his tailor. Georgiana was in her rooms with her governess, hard at her lessons. Fitzwilliam and Elizabeth were, of course, still honeymooning in their rooms. They had not come down for breakfast this day.

The maids were taking this opportunity to give the public rooms a thorough cleaning, under the supervision of Mrs. Baxter, the Darcy's devoted housekeeper and wife to the butler. That couple was taking a well-deserved break for a cup of tea together in the office they shared. Suddenly, the peace of the house was shattered when a maid came rushing in to explain that, in answer to a knock on the door, one of the footmen opened it to a shrieking lady. Mr. Baxter quickly made his way to the entryway.

"Where is my brother?" the lady demanded. "I must speak with him immediately on a matter of great urgency!"

The lady causing the fuss was Lady Catherine de Bourgh, George Darcy's sister-in-law. It was obvious to everyone in the vicinity that Lady Catherine was most seriously displeased.

Mr. Baxter bowed with all due solemnity. "I apologize, ma'am. Mr. Darcy is out this morning."

"Out? OUT? Where can he be? Why did he not await my arrival?" Lady Catherine did not really expect the butler to know the answers to her questions. "Since my brother is not available, I will speak with my nephew, immediately!"

Mr. Baxter was not about to interrupt Fitzwilliam and Elizabeth. Even without the master's edict that the couple was to be left completely alone and unavailable to visitors, the butler had too much affection and respect for the young couple to bother them during this time.

"I am sorry, ma'am, Mr. Fitzwilliam Darcy is also unavailable."

"What do you mean, **unavailable**? I am his aunt, nearly his closest relation. When I desire to speak to him, he is available to me," the great lady replied.

Mr. Baxter sighed to himself. He could see she was not going to make this easy for either of them.

"I am sorry, Your Ladyship. Neither the master nor his son are available to receive visitors this morning."

At this, Lady Catherine began a tirade, abusing Mr. Baxter for what she called his insubordination, and threatening his employment. The butler listened stoically, not giving Lady Catherine any hint of his emotions, and not at all worried at what she said. The lady was famous—**or infamous, rather**—for giving her opinion whether it was wanted or not, and for not letting facts get in the way.

As he knew she eventually would, Lady Catherine's volume and verbosity began to dwindle. Finally, she spat at him, "I will await one of them in the Blue Parlor. Whichever one arrives home first, I would speak to immediately. You will send refreshments to the room, as well."

With that, she turned, nose in the air, and marched to the aforementioned parlor. Once there, Lady Catherine chose the most imposing chair in the room and settled herself in to wait.

And wait she did. Two hours later, Darcy had not arrived home, and the butler insisted Fitzwilliam was unavailable.

"This is not to be borne!" Lady Catherine, in her frustration and anger, had begun to berate Mr. Baxter again when the master walked into the room.

"Catherine! You will cease this shrieking immediately! I could hear you from the front door; why are you standing in the parlor of my house, threatening my butler like the worst kind of fishwife?" Darcy knew very well why his sister-in-law was here, but he was not going to accept her typical behavior. Thankfully, his wife had been nothing like her sister. Their marriage would not have been the happy one it was if she had been.

At this, Lady Catherine closed her mouth with a snap. She was unused to being spoken to in this manner, but she had a great deal of respect for George Darcy. He was one of the few people to whom she would listen and obey. She sat back down, affronted that he had called her a fishwife, but unwilling to argue. She needed his cooperation in order to get her way. She looked at Darcy and began.

"You can be at no loss, Brother, to understand the reason I am here." Lady Catherine paused, as if waiting for Darcy to say something, but he would not oblige her.

"A most alarming report reached me yesterday, and I immediately set out to make my sentiments known to you." She hesitated, waiting to see if he would now respond. When he did not, she continued.

"Is it true, George Darcy, that you allowed your son, **my daughter's betrothed**, to marry another? And whom did he marry? Elizabeth Bennet? I have never heard of any Elizabeth Bennet! Who is she? What are her connections? Are you out of your head, allowing such nonsense?"

Lady Catherine was becoming more and more enraged. She began spewing vitriol at him. Darcy, in a similar manner to his butler, simply let the lady vent her spleen, knowing she would sooner or later wind down like a clock.

Once she had finished, Darcy began to speak. "Catherine, Elizabeth is the niece of my friend Gardiner. Before we continue this conversation, I will thank you for remembering that I will brook no disrespect towards him or his family." He paused to let his words sink into Catherine's head before he continued.

"I have never supported your notion of marrying Fitzwilliam to your Anne. She is too frail to stand up to the rigors of a Derbyshire winter, much less child-birth, and you know that is an im-portant consideration. My wife may or may not have conspired with you to betroth the two, but she never made mention of it to me.

"I have watched Elizabeth for many years and have long known that she and my son were a perfect match. Her father is a gentleman, and her uncle, tradesman or no, is one of my great-est friends.

"The deed is done, Catherine, and the marriage consummated. There is no point continuing this conversation. She is my daughter now, and under my protection and that of Fitzwilliam. You will accept her and the marriage or you will leave and not darken our door again until you do."

Lady Catherine looked as though she wanted to say something, to argue further, but knew it would be pointless. She gathered her dignity and tried to think of a way to remove herself from the house without severing an important connection. Lifting her chin, she replied, "I understand perfectly, Brother. You will hear no more from me. I must be on my way; I have a need to speak with the earl."

"By all means, go ahead and visit him, but be aware that he has been told the same things you have. He may give you a sympathetic ear, but he will not assist you.

"If you wish to meet your new niece, she and Fitzwilliam will be accepting callers in a few days. You may return then." He watched his sister-in-law march out the parlor door, calling for her carriage. He was not sure exactly where she stood or what thoughts were floating around in her head, but he was not concerned. Elizabeth had the backing of the family, not that she needed it, and none of Catherine's plans would injure him or his household. Not in society or anywhere else.

Darcy House, London

Eight days after the wedding

Fitzwilliam and Elizabeth came down to breakfast holding hands, as had become their custom. They were on time today, as their "honeymoon" was now over. Fitzwilliam was to attend a business meeting with his father, and Elizabeth was to begin learning from the housekeeper how Darcy House operated. Both had enjoyed their time together, and came away from the week feeling a closeness they both found they craved.

While the new couple had been spending time together, the Gardiners and George Darcy had been making decisions. Elizabeth's family knew they could not continue to impose on Darcy's hospitality. They were anxious about their safety and that of their children, but with Lizzy now safely married, they felt that they could and should go home. Darcy disagreed, and persuaded the couple to keep their family with his until Lizzy's honeymoon was over. They had reluctantly agreed to extend their stay a few days longer, and would be going home after breakfast today.

Darcy had received a report three days ago from the investigator following Lord Regis. The news was not encouraging. The peer had been visiting gambling halls and brothels, fighting at the least encouragement and abusing prostitutes. In addition, he had been heard by the investigators muttering imprecations about "penniless country chits" and "ungrateful little baggage," though thankfully not mentioning any names. Nothing had been reported by the investigator in regards to threats against the Gardiners or Johnson, who with his colleagues had been guarding their house all week. The report shared that the home had remained unmolested, as well. Gardiner and Darcy had concluded that it was likely safe for them to return.

The Darcy and Gardiner families enjoyed one last meal together before the Gardiners headed home. Conversation flowed easily amongst the group. The Gardiner children and Georgiana had joined the adults that morning, and the atmosphere was a cheerful one, despite the lingering sadness that resulted from the knowledge that the party was breaking up.

Maddie, Gardiner, and Darcy took this opportunity to observe Fitzwilliam and

Elizabeth. It was clear to all three of them that affection had grown between them. They frequently shared touches and smiles, seeming at times to almost communicate with only their eyes. Maddie resolved to speak to her niece before she left today; if what she suspected was true, Lizzy's concerns about her future happiness had been resolved.

Darcy, who knew his son better than the Gardiners did, could see that he was entirely besotted with his new wife. Gardiner was rapidly coming to the same conclusion, but unlike his wife was unable to see in Lizzy's behavior any indication of her feelings. That she held affection for him was obvious, given the touches she had given and received from her husband, though how deeply she held those emotions was not as obvious. Gardiner looked to his wife. Her expression communicated her awareness of his concerns, and he understood that she would be speaking to their niece in the course of the morning.

When the meal was complete, Elizabeth accompanied her aunt to the Gardiners' rooms to chat while Maddie supervised the packing of their belongings. The two spoke of inconsequential things for a while, until the trunks were packed and the servants dismissed. Then Aunt Maddie broached the topic uppermost in her mind.

"So how do you like married life, Lizzy?"

Elizabeth blushed, then laughed. "I like it very well. Your advice to relax and trust my husband was excellent. He was considerate, and it was a wonderful experience."

"And your feelings towards him? Have they undergone a change? Do you still have reservations? The two of you seem to be getting on very well."

"They have. I cannot say that all of my concerns have been allayed, but I am more hopeful now that we will be happy. Certainly, he is attentive to me to a degree I had never imagined possible. There is no need I have that he does not move heaven and earth to meet. His tenderness with me is heart-warming. I cannot say I am in love with him, at least not yet, but I can say that I might soon love him. My only desire is that he should share my feelings. I am not certain what would be worse, a total lack of love on both parts, or un-requited love on mine."

Maddie pulled her niece into a hug. "My dear, I think you have no worries on that score. Anyone can see the ad-oration in Fitzwilliam's eyes when he looks at you. I am sure he will soon declare it to you, but even if he does not, you must tell him when you are sure of your feelings. You do neither of you a service to hide yourself from him. Let him be your friend—your best friend. Share your heart and all your concerns with him. Communication will be the key to continued happiness in your marriage, regardless of your feelings or his. Promise me, Lizzy, that you will share your feelings with Fitzwilliam once you are sure of them." Maddie's voice was urgent.

Elizabeth felt all the importance of what her aunt was asking. "As soon as I am sure of my feelings, I will share them with Fitzwilliam. I promise."

"Thank you, Lizzy. You will not regret it."

Aunt and niece hugged each other tightly, before heading down the stairs to meet Gardiner and the children in the foyer. There, more hugs were given and received, and a slightly teary Elizabeth waved some of her dearest family members off. Fitzwilliam stood at her side, his hand at the small of her back, giving his support. When the

Gardiners had gone, Fitzwilliam walked with Elizabeth to the house-keeper's office, where she was to meet with Mrs. Baxter to begin her lessons regarding everything about running the house.

"Are you well, darling?" he asked.

Elizabeth smiled at him. "I am well," she answered. "It is time for us to begin our life together, and therefore time for my family to go back to theirs. I will miss them, but I have you and your family now, and I will be very busy learning to run this house. And, we will soon be attending balls and dinners and all that such events entail. I am quite sure I will be far too occu-pied to repine for my family. Too, they are not all that far away, and I can visit of a morning if I choose."

Fitzwilliam was relieved to hear this. He felt far less guilt about leaving her, knowing she was well. At six and ten, she was so young, and this would be her first day completely away from the family with whom she had grown up. True, she was intimately acquainted with him and his father and sister and had spent countless hours over the years in their company, but that was different than living here with them and away from those with whom she was even more familiar. With all the danger and anxiety his Elizabeth had suffered under in the last months, he did not want to add to it. His wish was for her to be always happy and safe.

"Well, then, my dearest wife, I will leave you for now. Father and I should be home before dinner. If you need anything at all, do not hesitate to let Mr. or Mrs. Baxter know. They will know how to reach us. Do not leave the house without Hooper and Duncan. I know you are an independent lady, but until Lord Regis has been dealt with, you are still in danger. Promise me, Elizabeth."

His wife looked aggrieved for a moment or two as he made his final statements, but agreed to his strictures. It was far better to be inconvenienced for a while longer than to be subject to **that gentleman's** attentions.

Chapter 9

Darcy House, London

The next day

Fitzwilliam Darcy strode through the hall and into the foyer heading to his father's study. Suddenly, he heard a familiar yet despised voice speaking to Mr. Baxter, causing him to halt. There, accompanied by the butler, was George Wickham, heading towards the study. **Must be short of cash,** thought Fitzwilliam cynically.

George Wickham was Mr. Darcy's godson and the son of Pemberley's steward. He had been, for all intents and purposes, raised with Fitzwilliam, and they had once been as close as brothers. Mr. Darcy took a great interest in George, and as a way of thanking the father for faithful service, he paid for the education of the son. It did not hurt that the two boys were close. He was greatly relieved that Fitzwilliam had a playmate near to his age. He had his cousins, of course, but they lived at the earl's estate and were not daily visitors. George, on the other hand, lived at Pemberley and was in company with Fitzwilliam daily. This apparently close friendship had persisted even into Eton and Cambridge.

What George Darcy had not known was that his son's playmate had a tendency toward viciousness, prevarication, and petty thievery. Once at University, those characteristics expanded to include debauchery and gambling to excess.

Fitzwilliam spent years covering for his friend's misdeeds, until an incident of cheating almost damaged **his** reputation. Wickham stole one of Fitzwilliam's essays and turned it in as his own. Thankfully for Fitzwilliam, another student—who had no love for

Wickham—saw the theft and reported it to the dean. Due to Wickham's connection to the Darcys, his punishment was light, and he went on his merry way no less out of countenance than when he had begun.

For Fitzwilliam, however, this was the end of covering up his **friend's** misdeeds. He quietly let it be known to his professors, friends, and close acquaintances that the connection between himself and Wickham was dissolved, and that any disputes they had with the gentleman needed to be taken to Wickham himself. Still, he did not tell his father what happened, nor that their friendship was at an end. He was always cordial to Wickham if he happened to be in when the other man came to the house; it was a small price to pay to keep his beloved papa happy.

"Darcy, how good to see you!" Wickham's face was spread with a smug grin. Truly, he did not think it was altogether good to see his childhood playmate, but one must maintain appearances. In Wickham's opinion, Fitzwilliam Darcy was austere and frigid. He was never interested in having a good time, or enjoying the benefits of a young gentleman of his station. In Wickham's mind, it was no surprise that old Darcy enjoyed his company over that of his own son.

Wickham had recently heard a rumor that Fitzwilliam had gotten married. He was sure that, if it were true, he would soon be able to pluck this new wife out from under his former friend's nose. He doubted the gentleman knew what his member was, much less what to do with it. The poor lady would no doubt be very lonely very soon and need comfort from a gentleman who most definitely knew what he was doing.

Wickham vividly remembered some of the arguments between Miss Elizabeth and Fitzwilliam; she had not seemed to like him much then. Perhaps she had married him for mercenary reasons. If this was the case, Wickham was even more likely to succeed with her.

Fitzwilliam responded stiffly, "Indeed." He did not trust George Wickham, but knew he needed to be polite. It would not do for Father to hear him being less than correct towards the gentleman.

As the two spoke, Elizabeth descended the staircase. Wickham noticed her first, as Fitzwilliam's back was to her, and greeted her as she stopped one stair from the bottom behind her husband.

"Miss Elizabeth! How good it is to see you! It has been an age; are you well? Is all your family here?" Wickham knew Lizzy had never quite trusted him. In fact, he laid the blame squarely at her feet for at least two youthful misadventures for which he was punished at Pemberley; she once found him and an upstairs maid in a closet, and another, earlier, time, she tattled to Mr. Darcy when she came upon him beating his horse for throwing him after a failed jump over a short hedge. She had grown up quite nicely, however, and he would not at all mind becoming intimate with her. He gave her a lecherous smile as he bent over her hand, which he had grasped from her side without her permission.

"Mr. Wickham," Elizabeth intoned. She had always been wary of George Wickham, and given her recent reticence following the debacle that was Lord Regis, she was even more so. There was something about Wickham that put her strongly in mind of the peer who was harassing her. The look in his eye today was most assuredly making her uncomfortable, and she vowed to herself to remain cautious when he was near. After retrieving her hand from the gentleman, she reached out for her husband.

Fitzwilliam turned around upon Wickham's greeting to his wife, grasping the hand she extended and smiling at her. He turned to his father's visitor and said, "You must wish us joy, Wickham. Elizabeth and I were married nine days ago. She is Mrs. Darcy now." He wanted his nemesis to clearly understand that Lizzy was under the protection of himself and his father. Fitzwilliam would not put it past his enemy to try to harm his wife. He knew Wickham's sins had gone far beyond the cheating and gambling he had covered for the gentleman. More than once Fitzwilliam found a home for one of Wickham's natural children, paying the mother off to remain quiet. No decent lady was safe from the other man's machinations. While he had never attempted anything with Elizabeth before, the temptation to revenge himself on Fitzwilliam by sullying his wife could very well be too great a one for Wickham to resist.

Wickham was both vexed and delighted. He did not like seeing his childhood playmate so happy. He knew Elizabeth had been a passionate girl, vigorously defending her ideas; surely that passion was still there. And given that she was now a married lady, he was positive her feelings were now channelled in better ways. He was even more certain now that he wanted to trifle with her, just to make Fitzwilliam miserable. He once again turned his smile towards Elizabeth.

"Indeed! I am quite delighted, Mrs. Darcy. You must allow me to congratulate you. Such a shame that you married such a boring gentleman. I'm sure you will soon be in need of some livelier companionship; I assure you I will always be available should you need a … **diversion**." Wickham raked his eyes up and down her form, that same lecherous grin on his lips, and winked at her, causing Lizzy to gasp in indignation. He was quite aware of the offense Fitzwilliam would take at this, but he was also aware that the gentleman would say nothing with his father in the vicinity.

"Never fear, Wickham, I am quite sure I will be keeping Mrs. Darcy sufficiently occupied. She shall have no need for your company, and neither shall I." Fitzwilliam was angry. How dare this rake come into his home and insult his wife?

"You will excuse us," he continued. "We have matters to discuss." With that, he placed his wife's hand on his arm and escorted her out of the foyer and into the parlor, shutting the door to ensure that Wickham did not follow.

Unbeknownst to the trio, Mr. Darcy saw and heard all that had transpired. His son did not know this, but another landowner, whose son attended Cambridge with Fitzwilliam, had told him of enough of Wickham's misadventures to give him pause. This same gentleman shared story after story of Darcy's beloved boy cleaning up Wickham's messes. Darcy had already determined he would speak with Wickham, making it clear that his future sponsorship depended upon good behavior and the taking of Holy Orders. Darcy had the living at Kympton in his gift and had promised his steward years ago that the gentleman's son would receive the living once it came open and after the boy took orders.

Of course, this was **before** he discovered Wickham's perfidy. He now felt it incumbent upon himself to make every effort to steer young George on the right path. If the young man continued as he was, his reputation, as well as Darcy's, would suffer and Darcy had no intentions of allowing his name to be dragged through the mud.

Darcy quietly made his way back to his study, arriving at the room just before Mr. Baxter knocked on the door and announced the visitor. He greeted his godson warmly, not allowing his countenance to display any of his anger and alarm. As much as he liked the boy, this was going to be a difficult interview.

An hour later, George Wickham barrelled out of Darcy House as though the devil himself were on his heels. **What happened to the old man?!** He had never spoken so in the past, lecturing Wickham on the proper behavior of a gentleman and threatening to end his support. Wickham was sure Fitzwilliam was behind it all. The prig probably came home from his Tour and told his father about every prank he had ever pulled, including that ill-fated cheating attempt. Blast it!

And there Fitzwilliam was, with a wife he likely did not know what to do with and more money and power than any one gentleman deserved. Of course, he did not actually **possess** the money and power, as his father was still living, but he **was** the heir. The old man could drop dead at any moment and there he would be, sitting on top of a pile of cash, several very nice estates, and a house in town. Not to mention a rather delectable lady who was at his beck and call.

And what did Wickham himself have? Not two shillings to rub together. His father was a steward. He had no legacy, no large inheritance to pass on to **his** son. No, **his** son was supposed to become a clergyman and spend his life listening to old ladies gossip and praying over sick and dying gentlemen. What a joke! As if he would ever do such things! No, Wickham had dreams that were superior to that. He intended to marry a rich lady and live a life of leisure. He planned to live his life the way Fitzwilliam Darcy was living his—with his every need well met and in a timely and opulent fashion. It was no less than what he deserved.

What escaped Wickham's notice—indeed, it had been escaping him for years—was that his father lived quite well on his income as Pemberley's steward. Mr. Darcy was exceedingly generous to his people, and to be hired to work at Pemberley was something. His generous salary, combined with the interest from a small income left to him by his own father, allowed the Wickham family to live, if not at leisure, at least with a solid roof over their heads and fine clothing. They did not want for anything.

However, Mrs. Wickham had been quite the spendthrift during her lifetime, which had ended when George was young. She had encouraged her son to aspire to lofty heights; loftier than he probably should have aspired. It was from his mother that Wickham learned his love of fine things, and it was from her that he inherited his ability to spend large sums of money quickly. He scoffed at his father's lectures on restraint and economy, preferring to strive for more. He did not understand how his parent could be happy in a subservient position, at another's beck and call, and forever required to be frugal.

Unfortunately, Wickham knew he had little recourse. He knew better than to offend his father's employer. He knew the two gentlemen—his father and old Mr. Darcy—were thick as thieves, and he was quite sure his father would hear about today's lecture. As much as he envied and disliked Fitzwilliam, he would have to control his impulses toward retribution. For now.

Later that night …

The Darcys were engaged that evening to dine with the Earl and Countess of Matlock. The couple had expressed mixed feelings about the betrothal of Fitzwilliam to Miss Elizabeth when Darcy told them of it. While they understood Darcy and Miss Elizabeth's uncle were friends, and that he would not tolerate disrespect toward any of that family, the fact remained that he had engaged his heir to the niece of a tradesman. It was simply not done! The upper class did not mingle with those of a lower station! However, because they had always been a close family, and knowing that George Darcy would approve of nothing that would damage his name or the name of Fitzwilliam, they agreed to reserve judgement until they met the girl. They wished the families to remain tightly-knit and for the Darcys to always feel able to be open with them, and vice versa.

Accordingly, they planned a family dinner as a way for the two families to become acquainted. The dinner had originally been meant to occur a few days ago, but the sudden wedding delayed it. Now that the pair had completed their honeymoon week, the invitation was re-issued and the evening anticipated with equal measures of curiosity, anxiety, and reluctance. Though still hesitant to approve of their new niece, family unity required it. They could only hope she was not overly gauche or absurd.

To the Matlocks' great relief, the new Mrs. Darcy was a charming young lady. She had a disarming smile and a sweet manner. She seemed a little timid at first, but Darcy explained some of her history to them, and they understood that it was not her usual way. Indeed, as the evening wore on and Elizabeth began to relax, her personality began to shine through her timorous behavior. Her impishness and slightly impertinent manner made the earl smile in delight. Truly, it seemed Darcy had chosen well for his son.

Fitzwilliam was clearly besotted with his new wife. The countess and her spouse had more than once exchanged astonished glances upon observing the smiles and joviality expressed by their normally quite serious and sober nephew. They did not have much previous knowledge of the new Mrs. Darcy and her habits, but she certainly gazed upon her new husband quite frequently with a great deal of affection.

When it came time for the party to separate after the meal, the ladies repaired to the drawing room, while the gentlemen remained in the dining room to enjoy brandy and cigars. The earl and his wife had earlier decided between themselves to question the new couple during this period of segregation in an effort to understand the union and how it came about. They were curious for the most part, but wanted as much information as possible before they gave their final approval, for their own peace of mind.

As a result, once drinks had been handed around, the earl began asking his nephew questions.

"So, Fitzwilliam, tell me of your bride. This marriage was arranged by your father, yet the two of you seem quite besotted with each other. How did you make her fall in love with you in such a short period of time? Your father has told me how reluctant she was at first."

Fitzwilliam blushed. "I am not sure that she is besotted with me, Uncle, but I will attempt to satisfy your curiosity." He glanced at his father for a moment, seeing his mouth twist in a slight smirk. He took a deep breath before beginning his story.

"I had determined upon agreeing to the match that I would do everything I could to make the betrothal as pleasant and romantic as possible for Elizabeth. I have always liked her very much and felt that she deserved more than a cold proposal and betrothal. With that in mind, I spoke of my hopes and reassured her of my fidelity and affection when I proposed. I could see immediately that she appreciated it, and responded accordingly.

"I knew as soon as I saw her in the parlor that day that she was distressed. Her eyes lacked the sparkle I had always associated with them, though her smile was just as sweet as ever. I observed her anxiety increase when mention was made of dinner at our home, and I made it my mission to put her at ease. I knew that while Elizabeth had agreed to the marriage, she had reservations. I knew if I wanted a happy life, I needed to court her.

"During our courtship, brief though it was, I spent as much time with her as possible. We went to the theater one night." Fitzwilliam smiled at the sweet memory.

"I had decided to woo her, but really had no idea how one went about it. I found that night at the theatre that I rather liked to be close to her, and being close to her in the dark was all the better. Not that I planned to ignore propriety, at least not completely. I was rather hoping she might not object to my holding her hand. We all found our seats in the box, and I was determined to sit beside her, which I was easily able to do." He lifted his eyes from the glass of port in his hand when his father chuckled.

"Elizabeth did not object when I grasped her hand, turning hers over to thread her fingers with mine. I took heart from her actions; perhaps ours might be a marriage of at least mutual affection, even if we never grew to love one another.

"Even before the trip to the theater, Elizabeth and I had been in each other's presence daily. I brought her small gifts, like flowers and books, and we walked frequently in the park near the Gardiners' home. We conversed on every topic we could think of and found that our characters and interests were more similar than we had previously believed. Her mind is so quick! She was able to grasp ideas and draw conclusions that I never thought a lady could. With the barest of information about a theory, she would begin to question and challenge me, going so far as to take a position on an idea that was in complete opposition to her true feelings on the matter.

"Every conversation with Elizabeth is an adventure. I look forward to hearing the next bit of wisdom drop from her lips. I have never met a lady such as she. My heart pounds to think of it! And the teases! My Elizabeth is ever teasing me, quite subtly, and despite the unease and distress she frequently feels. A gentleman could search the world over without ever finding another lady to match her for wit and intelligence. I feel blessed to have found such a treasure.

"I believe that I have made great inroads into making my wife love me as much as I love her, but I do not intend to stop wooing her. I find that I enjoy her, spending time with her and giving her gifts. Elizabeth is not the least bit mercenary, often taking me to task for overspending my allowance, which of course I am not. I like that she teases me a bit. She will one day be a wonderful mistress of Pemberley." Fitzwilliam smiled softly, the love for his new wife clear on his face.

Darcy addressed his son, "My boy, I agree wholeheartedly. I believe, though, that she already loves you. She may not realize it fully yet, but it is there for the rest of the world to see. Trust me in this, Son."

The earl nodded in agreement, and the gentlemen lifted their glasses in a toast. "To Mrs. Darcy."

The earl was satisfied that he had garnered enough information to please his wife. She would be vastly pleased with the intelligence he had gathered and he was eager to learn what she had discovered, as well. Accordingly, he turned the conversation to another topic.

Meanwhile, in the drawing room, the countess and her female guest were enjoying a quiet chat along similar lines. Lady Matlock found that the more she spoke with Elizabeth, the more she liked the girl. She knew her sister, Lady Catherine, was opposed to the match still, but the countess was not about to let that bother her. In fact, she would not at all mind tweaking Catherine's nose about it, and the best way to do that was to give Elizabeth a ringing endorsement in society. To that end, she arranged a shopping excursion with her new niece for the morrow.

Later that evening, after the Darcys had gone home, the countess and her husband shared with each other what they had learned. Both were impressed with Elizabeth, and agreed that Lady Matlock should be the girl's sponsor for her presentation at court, and that she should begin to introduce their new niece to her friends. The shopping trip tomorrow would be just the beginning. The Matlocks would hold a ball in her honor, as well as a few smaller gatherings. The couple went to sleep with their minds far more at ease than they had been previously.

Chapter 10

The next day ...

Elizabeth and Fitzwilliam stood in the foyer, while the footman retrieved Elizabeth's pelisse and bonnet in preparation for her shopping trip with Lady Matlock. The goal for today was to outfit Lizzy from head to toe. While they were at it, Lady Matlock was making sure that all of her friends were introduced to the newest family member.

The countess had sent notes around to all her dearest friends that she would be out with her new niece, and during the course of the day they all met at one or another of the many shops that the pair visited. Word quickly spread amongst the members of the **ton** that the new Mrs. Darcy was out and about, and Elizabeth was introduced to more people than she could ever remember.

Praise for the young lady was passed along from person to person in the sharing of the information. It was almost universally agreed that she was charming and witty, with pleasing manners. Some noticed her reticence, but few made notice of it, and most expected that Fitzwilliam Darcy would choose someone as reticent as he himself was. Of course, none of her new acquaintances knew of the events that led to Lizzy's reserve, nor did they know her before those incidents had happened. They were not aware of her liveliness; however, she did make a most favorable impression on the majority of those she met, and she received many promises of invitations to soirees of all sorts.

Unfortunately, one of the people who heard the news was the one person in London that Lizzy did not want to see.

Lord Regis was visiting his club, enjoying a few drinks with some companions, when he overheard two other members discussing some lady they had been introduced to while visiting the warehouses with their wives. He paid little heed until he heard the name Darcy. He began to pay more attention to their conversation, soon learning the general area where the party might be found. He quickly headed for the exit, determined to have his way.

While Lord Regis was gathering information and heading out the door of his club, Elizabeth and her aunt-in-law had made a final stop at a small bookshop that the Darcy gentlemen favored. The store specialized in older, hard-to-find volumes, though it also carried newer ones. Due to the special nature of the stock it carried, the shop was usually empty except for the proprietor, and today was no exception. The owner came out of the back room to greet the ladies before returning to the task he had been completing. The ladies were to meet the earl, Darcy, and Fitzwilliam here before heading to Matlock House to dine.

Upon entering the store, Lady Matlock and Elizabeth immediately headed to the back, near the poetry, where there was an area set up with chairs and a small table for customers to sit and peruse the merchandise. Before sitting down, they quietly browsed the books, each looking for something she thought her husband might enjoy. Elizabeth found two volumes she thought Fitzwilliam would like. She smiled to herself, thinking how good it made her feel to find something to please him. Making their selections, they sat to read something of them while waiting for the gentlemen to arrive.

Robert, the footman assigned to escort the ladies, stood quietly against the wall, eyes scanning the room. Mr. Darcy had been specific in his instructions, Master Fitzwilliam more so. He was to remain no more than ten feet from Mrs. Darcy at all times, and to intercede should **any** gentleman approach her.

Soon the ladies heard the ringing of the store's bell and looked up to see if it was their gentlemen who entered the store. It was a short minute or so later that Elizabeth was standing in dread. Lady Matlock, upon seeing Elizabeth's face suddenly pale, rose with her. Robert quickly stepped to move between his mistress and the red-faced gentleman, but he was not quick enough. The gentleman had shoved him out of the way and grabbed Mrs. Darcy's arm almost before he could think.

Upon leaving his club, Lord Regis had quickly made his way to the area along Old Bond Street he had heard mentioned. He knew Elizabeth was in one of these shops, and he also knew, from listening in on a conversation or two, that she and her aunt were unaccompanied by their menfolk.

Lord Regis was quickly able to track the ladies down with a few well-placed questions, and soon entered the bookshop at which they were waiting. He could see Elizabeth almost as soon as he entered, as she sat in the back of the shop, and the sight of her enraged him. He charged down the aisle, smiling to himself in grim satisfaction when he saw her skin pale at the sight of him. He grabbed her arm when he got close enough, shoving the footman out of the way when he tried to move between them.

"Elizabeth, fancy meeting you here," Lord Regis ground out.

Before Elizabeth could respond, Lady Matlock, who had arisen when the younger woman did, spoke to Regis, "Unhand my niece, sir! Who do you think you are to accost us here?"

Lady Matlock had never met Lord Regis, but knew this could not be anyone else. She reached for Elizabeth's other arm, determined to assist in any way she could.

Regis, upon looking around and ascertaining that no one else was in the shop, at least not within hearing or seeing distance, sneered at the woman who challenged him. "Who do you think you are, madam? I have business with this young lady. Do not get in my way; it is none of your concern. Remove yourself or I will take pleasure in removing you."

By now, Robert had recovered his wits enough to at least decide on his next step. He could see that the gentleman holding Mrs. Darcy's arm was very angry, and that his grip was causing her pain. Even worse was the abject fear he saw in her eyes. Out of the corner of his eye, he saw his master and Lord Matlock pass the window of the shop, and quickly made his way to the door.

When Darcy, his brother, and his son entered and saw the footman rushing towards them, they became alarmed. Robert knew his orders, and was not one to disregard them. Quickly Mr. Darcy inquired of the servant what the matter was.

Upon his footman's almost breathless statement that a gentleman had accosted Mrs. Darcy, Fitzwilliam went charging down the length of the bookshop followed quickly by his father and uncle. When he saw the fear, pain, and distress in his wife's tear-filled eyes, he rushed toward the trio. The shop's owner had come out to greet the newcomers, but seeing the sudden anger in their faces, quickly ducked back into his work room. He did not want to be caught up in the affairs of the Quality, and as he did not believe in gossiping, he did not want to know what was happening in the far reaches of his shop.

For Elizabeth, the mere sight of the peer who had turned her life upside down was upsetting. To have his hands on her person was almost more than she could take, and she responded instinctually, lashing out the only way she could with both arms held as they were. Before she even thought through what she was doing, she stomped her assailant's foot as hard as she could, then brought her knee upwards. She had discovered quite on accident, during a tickling session that had turned into a bout of wrestling with her new husband, that gentlemen are very sensitive in their most private area. Instinctively, she knew that he would likely let go of her arm if she struck him there. Unfortunately, her angle was wrong, and she only grazed him. This, in turn, made the gentleman angrier, resulting in his stronger grip on her arm as he shook her then slapped her face with his open hand.

Despite the pain and fear coursing through Elizabeth, she was also angry. Who did this gentleman think he was to treat her so? She was more glad than ever that she had turned down his proposals. Once again she realized how terrible her life would have been had she tied herself to him. Certainly it would not be the happy one she now had with Fitzwilliam.

And where was Fitzwilliam? He and his father should have arrived at the bookshop by now. Elizabeth knew she would be safe once they were in the building, but she did not know what to do in the meantime. Suddenly, the point became moot as Lord Regis was ripped away from her.

Unfortunately for Lord Regis, his slap of Mrs. Darcy was seen by young Mr. Darcy, who was all the more enraged at the sight. Peer or no, Regis was about to pay for his abuse of a Darcy wife.

Lord Regis had not registered the sound of the shop's bell ringing when the gentlemen had entered and so was not prepared to be interrupted. Suddenly, he was pulled backwards and a hand was at his throat, squeezing tightly and choking the breath out of him. Fitzwilliam Darcy stood before him, stiff and angry, nose-to-nose and snarling at him.

"Unhand my wife!" Fitzwilliam growled at the peer, rage turning his normally serious mien into a hard, granite-like mask. In his surprise, Regis let go of Elizabeth, who immediately collapsed into a heap on the floor.

Lord Matlock and Darcy entered the sitting area just behind Fitzwilliam,

Matlock heading straight for his wife, and Darcy pulling his son away from Lord Regis.

"Let me handle this, Son. See to Mrs. Darcy; she is unwell."

At this, Fitzwilliam's head whipped around, seeing for the first time his wife crumpled on the floor. He let go of the peer and quickly stepped to Elizabeth, bending down to tenderly pull her into his arms. After quietly crooning to her for a few minutes, he helped her to rise, informing his aunt and uncle that he was taking her to the carriage. They nodded their approval, choosing to stay and witness Darcy's confrontation with the lord.

Lord Matlock had been greatly relieved to find his wife unharmed, after seeing the grip Regis had on Elizabeth. After ascertaining that she had no injuries, and giving his approval to Fitzwilliam to take Elizabeth outside,

Matlock gave his total attention to his brother.

Once Fitzwilliam had let Lord Regis go, the peer had stumbled backward, his hands going to his throat as though to protect it from further attack. He coughed and gasped as his lungs filled once again with air. All he could think about at this point was survival; thoughts of his target were all but forgot. Therefore, it was with no little surprise that he was suddenly confronted with a very angry George Darcy.

"Lord Regis," Darcy sneered, looking down his nose at his opponent. "I would say that it is a pleasure to see you if I did not have such a great disgust for you."

Lord Regis may have been a peer, but George Darcy was a very powerful man, despite his lack of a title. Regis had never had much respect for the gentleman himself; in fact, he considered him an uptight, overly moralistic fellow. Darcy never participated in the typical diversions available to one of his class, something that Regis himself did quite frequently. However, Darcy was also known and honored for his honesty and discernment. He was highly regarded amongst the **ton** and the nobility and had the power to ruin anyone he chose, especially with the support of the House of Matlock. Regis therefore looked warily at his adversary, but chose to speak fearlessly.

"What do you want, Darcy? You and your son have interfered enough in my business. That girl belongs to me. **Me**. I want what is mine."

Darcy laughed derisively. "It is far too late for that, **sir**. She is a Darcy now, and under the protection of the Darcy and Fitzwilliam families. The marriage between my daughter and son cannot be undone. You know this. Any plans you might have had for her would have had to be completed covertly; you would not have only ruined her reputation had anyone seen you accost her here, you would have ruined your own. If it had not been so hurtful to my son's wife, I would have happily let you ruin yourself right here, in public. However, it *was* hurtful to her. You are aware, are you not, that my son was enraged to find you touching his wife? And you are also aware, I am sure, that had I not stopped him, you would likely be either dead or called out and facing him on the field of honor?"

Regis' hand went back to his throat. Indeed, he was aware of both facts. He swallowed again as Darcy continued.

"I have had you investigated, Regis. I am aware of the full extent of your gambling debts. I am also aware of the beatings you give people when you are angry, either at your preferred pugilists' establishment, at your favorite brothels, even at your own home to your servants and family members. You, sir, are a savage and a ruffian, and not worthy to bear the title of gentleman. I lay before you a choice: you may persist in your persecution of my daughter and her family, and I will destroy you; or, you may desist and remove yourself from our vicinity and spare your family and yourself the humiliation of the scandal that would surely follow were I to spread the word of your activities."

Lord Regis knew that Darcy was not a man to make idle threats. The ache in his throat and neck were enough to remind him that he should think twice before angering him or his son.

In truth, Regis was a bully. His mother had coddled him as a child, always giving in to his whims and temper tantrums and never making the effort to train her beloved son in the proper way to behave. As he had grown older, she had grown more and more afraid of him. It was too late to change him, however, and so she continued the pattern she had started so many years ago, giving him anything he wanted.

Prior to meeting Elizabeth, Regis had never been rejected. He had been shocked when she turned down his proposal, and had reacted as he always had, assured such actions would get him what he wanted. When her father banished him from the property, he had gone behind the man's back, colluding with Mrs. Bennet to compromise Elizabeth as soon as she was well. He had waited in Hertfordshire for weeks for Elizabeth to come back out in society. He had been determined to have her.

His anger when he discovered her removal from Longbourn had been terrible. He had rushed back to London, determined to find her and make her his. He did not love Elizabeth; he wanted to possess her. And he always got what he wanted. This desire is what led to his entrance into her uncle's house in the middle of the night, and it was what led him to this bookstore today.

But like all bullies, Lord Regis was thwarted when someone stronger than he stood up to him as Darcy had just done. He may be a peer, but Regis still had to live by society's rules, and much of his behavior in private would not stand up to the light of day. He could not afford a scandal to damage his reputation and that of his family. He had siblings that still needed to be married off, and the power that he was garnering in the House of Lords would wane if any hint of his misdeeds with women or his gambling debts were to reach his peers in Parliament. And, while his mother and siblings would do what he told them, he did not wish to deal with the aggravation of their whining.

"Indeed, Darcy," he sneered in an attempt to retain some small portion of his dignity. "I will accede to your demands. Your son may have the intemperate, beggarly little chit. She is no longer worthy of my notice, having given herself over to such a priggish family. You and the little baggage will hear no more from me, nor will her family."

"See to it that none of us do, Regis. For I am sincere in what I said. I will ruin you and your family if I see you anywhere near. Leave, and know that I will have you followed and will know if you leave town or stay."

Lord Regis bowed shallowly to Darcy, turned on his heel, and strode out of the shop. As he passed the Darcy carriage, distinguishable by the crest on the door, he paused for a second, then immediately resumed his march up the street. He hailed a hackney to take him home, where he informed his family and servants of their imminent departure before he walked up the stairs to his rooms and proceeded to drink the first of several bottles of brandy.

Back at the shop, the Matlocks congratulated Darcy on his handling of the peer before the three of them paid for the ladies' purchases and boarded the Darcy carriage for the trip home. Inside the equipage, they found Fitzwilliam and Elizabeth on the same seat, tightly entwined, with Fitzwilliam's cheek resting on her head. Elizabeth made to move to the other side, but her husband refused to let her go, raising his head and giving his family a look that defied them to remark on the situation. None thought it wise to do so, silently filling the other seat before Darcy banged on the roof to let the coachman know to proceed.

Fitzwilliam had managed to calm Lizzy after her confrontation, though he himself was still angry. He was relieved to hear from his father the details of the conversation that took place in the shop between his father and Regis. Elizabeth was also greatly comforted with the knowledge that her tormentor was leaving town and had promised to leave her and her family alone. She felt as though a great weight had been lifted from her shoulders. As exhausted as she was from fear and tears, she managed a glowing smile that took her husband's breath away.

The coachman drove the group first to Matlock House to drop off the earl and countess, before heading back to Darcy House. Upon disembarking the carriage, Darcy spoke to Robert, thanking him for his quick thinking. Even though he had been unable to prevent Lord Regis from accosting Elizabeth, Robert had gotten to the gentlemen quickly enough that they were able to stop the man. Thankfully, there had been no other customers in the shop, and after being passed a gold sovereign, the proprietor had agreed he had seen nothing. There should be no gossip from the event that Regis himself did not generate, and Darcy knew how to handle that, should it happen.

Fitzwilliam disembarked after his father, turning to hand Elizabeth down. He immediately escorted her into the house and up the stairs, calling for bathwater to be sent to their dressing room. The couple had enjoyed their little suite of rooms so much that they had decided to make it their permanent chambers. Her abigail and his valet had worked out a system by which both had the time they needed to attend to their duties, so all were pleased with the outcome. Once at Pemberley, the couple would have separate dressing rooms, of course, but here in town it was far more intimate.

Upon reaching their rooms, Fitzwilliam began helping his wife remove her clothes and don her dressing gown to await her bath. After pulling her long-sleeved dress down, he saw the deep bruising left by Lord Regis on Elizabeth's delicate arm, and his rage returned. He clamped his lips together tightly so that none of the anger would get out and affect Lizzy. She had been through enough. However, he vowed to speak to his father further.

Once Elizabeth was in her dressing gown, Fitzwilliam also undressed and donned his. He intended to help her in her bath, so once the tub had been filled, he dismissed the servants. He settled first into the tub, then guided Lizzy to sit in front of him. He ran the soapy cloth over her body, being especially careful with her arm. He then quickly washed himself and rinsed them both before leaning back against the side of the tub and holding his wife close against himself.

Elizabeth enjoyed her husband's attentions, knowing that it was his way of expressing his care for her. As she lay in his arms in the warm water, she recalled the surge of emotion she had felt when he pulled her from the floor in the bookshop earlier in the day. She had not been sure in the moment what she felt and under the circumstances, she was not able to analyse it overmuch. Now that they were home and quiet and relaxing, she pulled that memory out and began to examine the feelings that had engulfed her in that moment. As she thought, she came to a startling revelation. **I am in love with him.**

"When did this happen?" she asked herself. She began to think back over the last fortnight or so—their week of courting, the terribly frightening night she fled to Darcy House, the wedding the next morning and the week of honeymooning. She began to realize that the fear and anxiety she had felt in regards to Lord Regis had clouded her every thought and action, disguising her true feelings towards Fitzwilliam.

In truth, she realized, she had been in love with her husband for quite a while. She was not at all positive she could say exactly when it had happened, but happen it had, and the feeling was wonderful. He really was the best gentleman she had ever known; in fact, he was perfect for her. He met every qualification she desired in a spouse: he respected her, treated her with affection and care, and was eager to discuss everything imaginable with her. Yes, she most definitely loved him!

She smiled at the thought and savored it for a few minutes before recalling her promise to her Aunt Maddie to tell Fitzwilliam as soon as she was sure of her heart.

"Fitzwilliam."

"Mmmmm," he replied, nuzzling her hair. "Yes, my love?"

"Fitzwilliam … I love you."

Her husband suddenly became very still, his heart pounding in his chest so hard she could feel it as she lay against him. "Say that again," he demanded in a whisper.

She adjusted her position so she could look over her shoulder into his face. "I love you. Very much."

"Oh my love," he breathed. "You do not know how I have longed to hear you say that. I love you, as well, my darling Lizzy." Both hearts soared with the knowledge that theirs would indeed be a marriage filled with love. Fitzwilliam leaned forward and kissed his beautiful wife. Soon all thoughts left their minds, their focus being only on each other and the increased pleasure that a union with one you loved and who loved you could bring.

Turn the page for an overview of the next book in the series, *Promises Kept* …

An Overview

of

Promises Kept ...

Darcy House, London

One year later

In the Master's study, Darcy leaned back in his chair, contemplating the discussion he had just had with his steward, John Wickham. Darcy and Wickham were on very good terms, and always had been. There was a great similarity of mind between them in the matters of managing the estate, and Wickham was a diligent and excellent steward. The two were as close as servant and master could be.

Darcy's sponsorship of the son in his education was a direct result of the respect he felt for the father.

The two had just concluded a painful interview about young George. Darcy returned home unexpectedly late one morning after realizing he had forgotten some important papers he needed for the meeting he was headed to. He opened the door of his study that fateful day to find his godson, pockets full of small, saleable items from the house, trying to pick the lock on the strongbox that contained the household funds. The young man tried to talk his way out of the situation, and Darcy may have let him go with a word of warning had he not realized that the young man needed to learn a lesson. Instead of letting him go, Darcy called the constable and George was hauled off to Newgate. Darcy hoped that the experience would frighten his godson a bit, and cause him to think before he acted the next time he considered an illegal activity.

Darcy had immediately written to John Wickham, asking him to come to London. While Wickham was travelling, Darcy made sure that funds were available at the prison for food and other necessities for George. He had not felt so badly about anything he had done in years.

The interview with his steward had been difficult, but Wickham shared with him that he had heard rumors of his son's behavior in the past and was understanding of the circumstances. He expressed devastation, of course, that his only son would do something so heinous. He shared that had seen the boy's longing for the finer things, as well as his disdain for what his father could give him, and spent years fearing for George, praying that George would be accepting of his place in society.

Darcy knew it broke Wickham's heart that his only child would steal and behave as a rake. He knew that the boy would have to pay whatever price came with his actions. A thief who had stolen as much as young Wickham had could hang. Neither man wanted to see that happen, now or in the future. Between them, the elder gentlemen decided upon a course of action that they hoped would teach young George to appreciate what he was given.

George Wickham would be sent to Canada, with the proviso that he not come back to England. If he should return, he would be faced with the punishment he would receive if Darcy pressed charges. Father and godfather both hoped he would embrace this opportunity. John Wickham would speak to his son about it, and Darcy would visit the judge. Darcy was a powerful man, and knew the judge would agree with the plan.

And so, a couple weeks later, George Wickham boarded a ship bound for Canada, his father's admonitions ringing in his ears, grateful that his life was spared. Certainly, going to a wilderness so far away was not appealing, but neither was hanging by the neck until dead!

~~~***~~~

Fitzwilliam Darcy was a happy man. Today was the first anniversary of his marriage to his beautiful Elizabeth, and the gift she had given him when he awoke thrilled him to the bone. He was going to be a father! He, Fitzwilliam Darcy, heir to Pemberley and half of Derbyshire, was going to be a **father**! Elizabeth had been sick for weeks, and that had worried him immensely, but she felt the baby quicken this morning and immediately shared the news with him. He had been disappointed that he was not able to feel it yet, but was assured by his lovely wife, who got her in-
~~~

formation from her Aunt Gardiner, that he would soon have that pleasure. Fitzwilliam grinned widely, remembering the thank you he had bestowed on his spouse and best friend.

Contemplating further, he reflected on the changes the year had brought, especially to himself and the way he responded to those with whom he interacted. Elizabeth had shown him defects in his character to which he had previously been oblivious. When his own father had taken her side in the matter, he knew she was not exaggerating and began to amend his behavior. Aside from his father's opinion, which he valued highly, his wife's was of paramount importance to him. She had proven herself over and over that she was no simple, unintelligent country girl. No, his Elizabeth was charming and witty, with an intelligence that at the very least matched his, if not at times surpassed it; she was a lady who deserved only the best. He strove daily to be worthy of her.

~~~***~~~

In another area of the house, Elizabeth was also contemplating the past year as she rested before tea. She was deliriously happy with her marriage, new family, and coming child. Fitzwilliam's father—Papa George, she called him—was everything she could wish for. He had opened her eyes to what an involved father did and said. While she still loved her own father deeply, she now recognized his errors in regards to his estate and family. In her letters, she encouraged him to take measures to improve her sisters' dowries and to educate the younger girls. She was unsure if her words made a difference, but felt she needed to try.

Elizabeth also wrote to her mother about the new society in which she
~~~

moved, warning her about her behavior and how it would affect her remaining, unmarried, daughters. Sometimes she used stories of things she had seen and heard to convey these warnings, and other times she stated things bluntly. Elizabeth and Mrs. Bennet would never have much of a relationship, she had come to realize. She loved her mother and chose to forgive her for her words and actions, but needed to keep her at arm's length for her own sanity.

Thinking of her maternal parent brought to mind the traumatic events that led to her marriage and the man that had caused them. Lord Regis had never bothered her again after the confrontation in the bookstore. He had all but disappeared from society events for the remainder of the season, though he attended to the House of Lords and his duties there with great diligence. His remaining single siblings had gotten married in the spring. His mother had passed in early summer, of apoplexy if rumors were to be believed. Regis himself had reportedly taken himself off to one of his estates, near Dumfries in Scotland, immediately following her funeral, where he met and married a local gentleman's daughter before the first half of his mourning was over. Elizabeth shuddered to think what the poor girl's life was like.

Elizabeth herself felt much safer now, and more like she had before her nightmare began. The episode had changed her in many ways. She was now more careful about how she presented herself to people, and who she trusted. She was cautious, which had had never been before, and was still more reticent with strangers than she had been previously. Thankfully the fear that had plagued her was gone. She felt safe and incredibly loved by her husband and their extended family,

and it showed in the smile on her face
and the wit she displayed to others.

Before you go …

If you enjoyed this book, please consider leaving a review at the store where you purchased it.

Also, consider joining my mailing list at

https://mailchi.mp/ee42ccbc6409/zoeburtonsignup

~Zoe

About the Author

Zoe Burton first fell in love with Jane Austen in 2010, after seeing the 2005 version of **Pride and Prejudice** on television. While making her purchases of Miss Austen's novels, she discovered Jane Austen Fan Fiction; soon after that she discovered websites full of JAFF. Her life has never been the same. She began writing her own stories when she ran out of new ones to read.

Zoe lives in the snow-belt of Ohio. She is a Special Education Teacher in an online school, and has a passion for romance in general (**Pride and Prejudice** in particular) and stock car racing.

Connect with Zoe Burton

Email:

zoe@zoeburton.com

Facebook:

https://www.facebook.com/ZoeBurton
Books

https://www.facebook.com/groups/Bur
tonsBabes/

Pinterest:

https://www.pinterest.com/zoeburtona
uthor/

Instagram:

https://www.instagram.com/zoeburton author/

Website:

https://zoeburton.com

Join my mailing list:

https://mailchi.mp/ee42ccbc6409/zoeb urtonsignup

Support me at Patreon:

https://www.patreon.com/zoeburtonau thor

Me at Austen Authors:

http://austenauthors.net/zoe-burton/

More by Zoe Burton

Regency Single Titles:

I Promise To…

Lilacs & Lavender

Promises Kept

Bits of Ribbon and Lace

Decisions and Consequences

Mr. Darcy's Love

Darcy's Deal

The Essence of Love

Matches Made at Netherfield

Darcy's Perfect Present

Darcy's Surprise Betrothal

To Save Elizabeth

Darcy Overhears

Merry Christmas, Mr. Darcy!

Darcy's Secret Marriage

Darcy's Christmas Compromise

Darcy's Predicament

Darcy's Uneasy Betrothal

Darcy's Yuletide Wedding

Darcy's Unwanted Bride

Darcy's Favorite

Darcy's Christmas Scheme

Darcy's Christmas Ball

Victorian Romance:

A MUCH Later Meeting

Westerns:

Darcy's Bodie Mine

Bundles:

Darcy's Adventures

Forced to Wed

Promises

Mr. Darcy Finds Love (available exclusively to newsletter subscribers)

The Darcy Marriage Series Books 1-3

Mr. Darcy, My Hero

Coming Together

Christmas in Meryton

The Darcy Marriage Series:

Darcy's Wife Search

Lady Catherine Impedes

Caroline's Censure

Pride & Prejudice & Racecars

Darcy's Race to Love

Georgie's Redemption

Darcy's Caution